BETWEEN BROTHERS

BRENDA BARRETT

A Jamaica Treasures Book/November 2017

Published by Jamaica Treasures
Kingston, Jamaica

978-976-8247-60-5
Jamaica Treasures
P.O. Box 482
Kingston 19
Jamaica W.I.
www.fiwibooks.com

"That boy." His mother glanced at him. "I saw you looking at him earlier. You ever speak to him?"

"Which boy?" Preston frowned.

"Jordan, I think his name is..." Jennifer gritted her teeth as if it genuinely hurt her to say his name.

"We are in the same class," Preston said reluctantly.

Jennifer swallowed. "Same class? Why didn't you tell me? I could have gotten it sorted out!"

"It is fine, Mom." Preston looked at his mother quizzically. *Why was she so afraid of him being in contact with Jordan?* It must have crossed her mind that it would happen some time or the other. Portland was a small parish. They lived less than five minutes from each other in the same district of Drapers. They were the same age.

"It is not fine." Jennifer hissed, "Not fine. Do not become friends with that boy."

"But why?" Preston asked, genuinely puzzled. He had always accepted the fact that the mere mention of the other Wiley's got his mother in an agitated state but seeing Jordan these past couple of days; he was questioning what was so bad about him. He had not teased him today.

He could have, but he didn't. He had not even allowed his friends to participate. That accounted for something.

"He is an abomination... a terrible curse from God," Jennifer said feverishly. "His mother is an evil witch, and we will not accept his existence!"

ALSO BY BRENDA BARRETT

FULL CIRCLE
NEW BEGINNINGS
THE PREACHER AND THE PROSTITUTE
AFTER THE END
THE EMPTY HAMMOCK
THE PULL OF FREEDOM
REBOUND SERIES
THREE RIVERS SERIES
NEW SONG SERIES
BANCROFT SERIES
MAGNOLIA SISTERS SERIES
SCARLETT SERIES
WILEY BROTHERS SERIES

ABOUT THE AUTHOR

Books have always been a big part of life for Jamaican born Brenda Barrett, she reports that she gets withdrawal symptoms if she does not consume at least two books per week. That is all she can manage these days, as her days are filled with writing, a natural progression from her love of reading. Currently, Brenda has several novels on the market, she writes predominantly in the historical fiction, Christian fiction, comedy and romance genres.

Apart from writing fictional books, Brenda writes for her blogs blackhair101.com; where she gives hair care tips and fiwibooks.com, where she shares about her writing life.

You can connect with Brenda online at:
Brenda-Barrett.com
Twitter.com/AuthorWriterBB
Facebook.com/AuthorBrendaBarrett

Chapter One

September 1996

"**Y**ou are one of the Wiley boys?" The girl asked as she eyed him with interest. "There is another one over there." She hooked her thumb and indicated to the other side of the classroom where Jordan was laughing with his friends.

Outgoing Jordan. Always surrounded by an eager crowd.

Preston looked at that side of the classroom, and their eyes met. Jordan had a half smile on his face, and he nodded his head imperceptibly in acknowledgment of their connection.

Preston hurriedly looked away. It was going to be hard to avoid Jordan since they both attended the same high school and were in the same class.

"Has anybody ever told you that you two could be twins?"

"No!" Preston growled dismissively. He turned his body slightly away from the inquisitive girl so that she couldn't see the blatant lie on his face.

Of course, he had heard it before. The people in the community where they lived said it all the time. It was hard to avoid the comparisons. They both looked like their father, Joseph Wiley.

"Are you the rich one or the poor one?" The girl asked.

"That's none of your business." Preston bristled. "Why are you so nosy?"

"Because I am nosy," the girl smirked. "You are obviously the poor one. You are very touchy aren't you?"

Preston sat back in his chair and wished that the class would start already but the first official day of school was always chaotic. The teacher kept popping in and out to deal with something or the other.

That was why he was left at the mercy of this unapologetic torturer. He glanced at her notebook. It had her name on it, Summer B. Fallon.

He looked at her again and almost groaned at his mistake. She was watching him. Her eyes were bright with interest.

"How does it feel?" She started chatting again.

"How does what feel?" Preston scowled. He shifted in his seat uncomfortably.

"You know..." Summer leaned her head to one side like she was examining him thoroughly. "If you are the poor one, that means that your mother is the one that is loved. I heard the story from my grandmother. She lives in your neighborhood."

"She needs to mind her own business!" Preston growled. "Seriously!"

"But it's nowhere near as interesting as yours." Summer grinned. "Our business is humdrum. Besides, it's not only my granny that knows your story; everybody who lives in Portland has heard it at some time or the other.

"Your father, Joseph Wiley was practically paid by old Mr.

Riddley to marry his ugly daughter, Jennifer Riddley.

"At the time, Joseph Wiley was engaged to marry the local beauty, Hannah Kennedy. How am I doing so far?"

Preston looked at her balefully. He wanted to tell her to stop, but at the same time, he was curious as to what others said about his family.

What Summer had said so far was pretty accurate. Except for the part where she called his mother ugly.

His mother was not ugly. People could be so hurtful at times. He didn't know what on earth people were thinking when they called her ugly. Granted, she did not look like Hannah Kennedy. Few women could claim to look that good. However, his mom was beautiful in her own way.

"I am right aren't I?" Summer squealed and clapped her hand like she was in the middle of an exciting movie.

"Go on." Preston shrugged. "I want to hear what else you think you know about my family."

Summer eagerly pulled her chair closer to his. "I heard that Old Mr. Riddley paid off Joseph Wiley to marry his ugly spinster daughter and then handed over the supermarket for him to run. Joseph was poor and needed the money, and he did it, but he couldn't leave the love of his life, Hannah Kennedy. He loved her too much. Jennifer was for money and Hannah was for love."

Preston grimaced. That was a reasonably accurate description of the situation. The whole thing made his mother unhappy. She had only agreed to marry his father because she loved him shamelessly and she had not cared that he had loved someone else.

"And the rest is like one of them Bible stories," Summer cackled. "Jennifer and Hannah had children almost at the same time. If one woman got pregnant, the other one did as well. It was like they had a baby competition. They share

Joseph Wiley like in one of those African stories. Except, sharing him is not at all peaceful like it is in African tribes."

Preston didn't comment. Sharing was a loose term as it related to his father. His father had six sons: three from his mom and three from Hannah. He and his brothers, Walter and Saint, were not given the time and attention that Jordan, Guy, and Case got. Even though his dad lived with them in the same house, he spent his leisure time with his other family. They simply got the best of him because he loved them more.

"So where do you fall?" Summer asked staring at him with eyebrows raised. "You are like what, son number 1 or 2?"

Preston sighed and slumped in his seat. "I am my father's first child."

"Then that would make you one of the rich Wiley's." Summer opened her eyes wide, "How does it feel to be the son of the ugly unwanted wife?"

"Shut up!" Preston finally snapped. "My mother is not ugly! And as son number one I am not only the rich Wiley, but I am the legitimate Wiley. My parents had me in marriage!"

He said it louder than he intended. Quietness descended on the relatively noisy classroom.

"Sorry, Legitimate Rich Wiley." Summer smirked and moved her desk further away from him. "It must be great being you."

Preston held his head down after the outburst. He had glanced at Jordan after he said that and a kernel of shame was growing in the pit of his stomach. Jordan looked like someone had sucker punched him. His mouth was slightly opened in shock.

Words had power. Preston realized instantly, but what he just said wasn't just his fault.

The 'legitimate Wiley' story was his mother's constant

litany from the time he was old enough to understand his family's unique dynamics. And he had somehow absorbed her sermon and was even repeating it in public.

His mother had fanned the flames of resentment to his other brother's, forbidding him to speak to Jordan, even though they were the same age and lived in the same community.

They have no business being in this world. They are not true Wiley's. Those were his mother's words, not his. Her voice was in his head, and it had found wings and taken off from his mouth for all the class to hear.

Preston glanced over at Jordan again and then looked away, contrition rife in his heart. He did not truly mean it. He wasn't even sure what advantages being legitimate afforded him anyway. In his opinion, it did not make his father love them any more or give them any more attention.

To be honest, he had always wanted to have a relationship with the boy who looked so much like him. It had always been a secret desire. Of all the boys, he and Jordan looked most like their father. He often wondered what Jordan thought about him.

If he could take back his outburst, he would.

But he couldn't.

It was said and ingested. He felt Jordan's eyes on him, and he reluctantly and hesitantly met his.

It was no surprise when their eyes met. Hatred was blazing from Jordan's.

He shouldn't have said what he did. He had just made an enemy.

****

"You heard what the punk said?" Shawn whispered in Jordan's ear. "I am my father's first son and the legitimate

Wiley in his little upper crust accent. Why do all of the prep school kids speak like that?"

"I have no idea," Jordan muttered. "The more money, the more refined I guess."

"We should lay wait him after school and give him a beat down. Beat the accent out of him." Cody volunteered helpfully. "I can bet he fights like a girl."

"Yeah," Shawn giggled, "we could rearrange his face so that it doesn't look so much like yours. I don't like that he looks so much like you."

"He is three months older," Jordan shrugged, "so technically I look like him, he was born first."

Shawn snorted, "Just three months, that's nothing. There are three of us and only one him. We can take him after school, wipe that stupid smirk off his pretty face."

Jordan chuckled. "You think he's pretty?"

Shawn nodded. "Yes, very. He looks like Ginuwine except prettier."

"Which would mean," Shawn sighed dramatically, "that you are pretty too. I hope you grow out of it, being a pretty boy is not cool."

Jordan groaned. "You kill me."

He didn't know if he should laugh or cry at being called pretty. Any insult or compliment leveled at Preston's face could be assigned to him.

They looked like they were cut from the same cloth. Manufactured in the same factory. Their only difference was that Preston was lighter skinned than he was, because his mother was light, and Jordan was curly haired because his mother was Indian.

Everything else was Joseph Wiley. The high forehead, the hooded eyes, the short straight nose, the pronounced cheekbones and the full lips.

When he was younger, his mother would allow his hair to grow long, and people would mistake him for a girl. He wondered if Preston went through that.

But then again he didn't know anything much about Preston, except that he lived in the mansion on the hill just ten minutes from where he lived. They had a long winding driveway and a massive black gate to bar out any casual visitors and a sign on the gate, which said: "Trespassers will be prosecuted."

He had never dared to go up there even when he and Shawn were embarking on their adventurous explorations. He just knew that the house on the hill was where his father lived with his other family and he had to stay away.

His dad never spoke about his other life when he came over to visit, mainly because it upset his mother deeply but while they were alone playing ball or running errands his father would tell him little snippets about Preston and Walter and Saint. His three brothers with a different mother.

It was only after glimpsing Preston in his mother's car one morning being chauffeur driven to his private prep school that he had found out that Preston resembled him. It had shaken him up at the time. Until then, he had just heard about Preston, but at that moment he had become genuinely curious.

And he had been curious ever since. His mother had told him not to ask his father about them, but it was hard not to give in.

He wanted to know so many things, like why couldn't they play together. He never saw Preston or Walter or Saint, outside their house. They didn't play in the street like him and his cronies.

He didn't even see them outside the house. For the last year, his curiosity about them had been at fever pitch. He always went to Shawn's house because it had a clear view of their house. From there he could look for movement on their large manicured lawn.

They probably had an indoor play area or a spacious area at the back, he had concluded. *Unless their mother had them living in a cage.* He heard stories about her, Evil Miss Jennifer who was so cold she ate children for breakfast.

Jordan glanced at Preston who was looking fiercely down at his desk like something super interesting was on it.

It was the first time in his twelve years of life that he was actually seeing his own brother up close.

"Stop looking at him," Shawn whispered. "He is not to be pitied. He is to be beaten."

Jordan shook his head. "Not worth it. We are in high school now. No fights."

Shawn snarled. "I could take him alone."

"And I warned you to stop fighting my battles for me," Jordan said exasperation leaking in his voice. "You promised that you would act more civilized this year."

"When did I make that ridiculous promise?" Shawn grunted. "Was I smoking something?"

"You were." Jordan sighed and looked at Shawn. "You told me you would quit smoking and you would act like a girl."

"I am in khakis," Shawn smirked. "If I act like a girl the whole school will think I am gay. And I did quit smoking. I hadn't really started."

"You said it," Jordan murmured. "You probably were high."

Cody sniggered. "Does the school, I mean the administration, know that you are actually female?"

"No." Shawn shrugged. "I registered as a boy. As far as they are concerned I am a boy. Khakis are nicer than those uniform dresses. Besides, girls pay way more for uniforms than boys which is unfair and should be addressed. They have way more pieces of clothes to buy."

"How did your parents let you do this?" Cody asked in awe.

"My mother thinks it is a nice social experiment and my father says I can choose to wear whatever I want." Shawn shrugged, "whether I wear a dress or pants to school means nothing to him."

Jordan chuckled. Shawn could easily pass for a boy. She looked right at home in her khaki pants and tucked in shirt. She was slim and flat chested, with her hair in a buzz cut. It was even shorter than his.

Shawn had always been one of the boys. He thought of her as his other brother. They were born at the same hospital, the same year, just a few months apart. Their mothers were close friends.

They lived two houses down from his on Spring Street in Drapers. It was only normal that he and Shawn would be inseparable while growing up.

It was only last year that it dawned on him that Shawn really was a girl and therefore not really his brother from another mother, as he liked to think of her. He had never seen her in a dress or act in a manner that he would call girly until they had been in the middle of a fight a couple of weeks ago.

They had been beating down a high schooler for daring to pick mangoes on their turf when it occurred to him while Shawn was on the boy's back hanging onto his neck and squeezing with a well-practiced arm wrestle that she was a girl.

"She would make a pretty girl too." Jordan's mother always said.

But she was better as a boy, Jordan concluded of his best friend. She was his partner in crime and had an insatiable need for adventure. He couldn't count the number of scrapes they had gotten into together over the years.

He didn't need another brother his age.

He glanced at Preston, and definitely not Mr. First and Legitimate Wiley.

Jordan was quite fine. He had Shawn. She was probably a hundred times better than Preston at everything.

Jordan doubted that Preston could even climb a tree or play ball. *Maybe he couldn't swim, even though Drapers was so close to the sea. The* thought made Jordan smile. Preston may be the rich legitimate one, but he didn't have much of a life, did he?

It probably hurt his rich little sensibilities that he had to attend the local high school with all the regular people.

Titchfield High School was not a posh private school, it was government run, but it had the reputation of being the best in their region. Everybody chose Titchfield for his or her first choice, but only the students with the highest grades got in after the external examinations.

They made no exceptions for anyone. No strings could be pulled. His mother had drummed that in his head every day for all of last year when she wanted him to study.

That meant that Preston had been bright enough to get in.

He looked lonely sitting at his side of the room. Maybe his little friends from his fancy prep school had not made the cut. He would have to make a new set of friends.

He felt a slight pang of sympathy for him, and then it slowly died. He didn't care anyway. Preston meant nothing to him. He was just a boy. They had the same last name and shared the same father. That was all. He doubted that they would even cross paths in the future.

Chapter Two

He hated high school. Preston concluded after just one week in the place. He slumped into the front seat of the car when his mother came to pick him up and barely mumbled a good evening.

It was quite ironic, this hate for Titchfield since the high school founded in 1786 was situated on one of the prettiest school spots in Jamaica. It was located on what was previously a military barracks; the guns from the 16th century and two of the old buildings from that era were still there and still standing. And though that was fascinating, what was remarkable about Titchfield was that it was bordered by a white sand beach, just a few steps from the school wall.

His classroom overlooked the sea and some mountains in the distance. It was the kind of view that visitors to Jamaica paid good money to appreciate; at least that was what his father always said.

It was supposed to be the perfect place to learn.

Instead, he was finding everything so far to be a challenge.

"Why so glum, honey?" Jennifer asked brightly. "How was school today?"

"Okay," Preston mumbled. He didn't mean it though. It was less than okay. School was barely bearable.

At his old school, he had friends, and he was comfortable. They had civilized extracurricular activities like chess and violin.

At this school he felt like a fish out of water, none of his friends had made the cut for Titchfield, so he was alone. Everybody in his class knew each other from their old schools. They formed little clusters of friends in no time, picking up where they left off before the summer break, discussing stuff that they had done, and reminiscing about their previous times together.

Every day for the past week was quite clearly a friend fest, and he was not invited. He had his one chance at inclusion on the second day of school, and he had blown it. The boys in his class were sports mad. They had been going on and on about Jamaica's historical milestone, the first English speaking country in the Caribbean to qualify for the World Cup.

And they were just salivating at Jamaica's chance to watch the games in '98. They were discussing the players and their moves and what was going to happen next, and he had been quite literally bored out of his mind listening to them.

He had not expected that Ryan Bigby, the most sports-mad of the boys would actually address him directly; they had been doing a good job of ignoring him up until then.

"What do you play, Preston?"

At first, he hadn't reacted. He didn't know that Ryan knew his name.

"I am talking to you, Wiley!" Ryan had smirked.

"Oh, me?" Preston shrugged. "I play tennis."

"Tennis?" Ryan had widened his eyes and rounded his mouth as if he had just received shocking news.

The other boys had looked at him like he had morphed into another species.

"I meant what position in football." Ryan had choked out.

"I don't play football," Preston had said defensively. "I play tennis."

And then the laughing started.

His tennis playing was ridiculed for the whole day.

To make matters worse, Jordan was there. He had been in the group of football-mad boys. He and his friend Shawn seemed as if they played every position.

Preston had paid particular keen attention when Jordan spoke about the game. He played in the local community club, and he was something of a star. The other boys certainly seemed to think so. He could see them judging him as they looked between him and Jordan.

He played tennis and Jordan was a star football player. There was no doubt as to who was the odd Wiley out.

He tried to stay away from their conversations after that, but what could you do in a class that was not that big and had a disproportionate amount of boys to girls. He couldn't be seen discussing stuff with the girls either. He didn't want to be ridiculed for being too girly.

He was sitting in the corner of the class at break time and minding his own business when they started discussing dancehall music and some feud that was brewing.

One faction of the class was on the side of an artiste called Beenie Man, and the other faction was on the side of another artiste called Bounty Killer, and he was staring at them as they defended their favorite artistes passionately.

Even the girls were in on it and got worked up. Fingers

were pointed, people were getting into each other's faces, and insults were hurled from one group to the other. He had nothing to say. He had no idea who they were talking about or even the songs that they sang or deejayed or whatever it is that the men did.

His mother abhorred dancehall. She was a rock steady fan if she listened to Jamaican music at all.

Ryan had seen his disinterest in the conversation and had bellowed at the top of the mayhem and madness.

"Who do you prefer, Tennis Wiley, Beenie Man or Bounty Killer?"

All eyes were on him as the class quieted down. He had made up his mind not to answer.

What were they asking him for? He was the class pariah. Hadn't they teased him enough and written him off as strange for playing tennis.

Another boy had insisted that he answer.

"Answer the question, Tennis Wiley." This boy, Brian Marshall, he was slightly afraid of; he was huge and looked like a thug. He was probably much older than twelve or thirteen. He had facial hair.

Suddenly he had been the focus of everyone's attention, including people who weren't even involved in the music conversation.

Even Jordan who had been with his friends in their own corner giggling about some secret thing had looked over at him alertly as if his answer would be a life or death matter.

A stubborn, defiant streak had him straightening his spine in defiance. "I don't know who the artistes are that you are talking about. So I like neither. I love classical music. I prefer Vivaldi over Beethoven."

"Classical music?" Ryan had asked incredulously, "as in the horror movie tunes that they play on Sunday morning on

RJR?"

"That's right," Preston had said. He couldn't quite hide the disgust he had felt towards them in his tone, "Though I wouldn't call them horror movie tunes unless you are referring to Bach. Organ music can be a touch heavy, but for someone who has no ear for that kind of sound, I guess it would sound like that to you."

Brian Marshall was the first to hit the desk and bellow with laughter. The rest of them followed.

"Remember what the social studies teacher said today about the 'b' word people, how they distinguish themselves from the working class?" Ryan asked gleefully.

"I think the word is bourgeoisie," one of the girls answered.

"Tennis Wiley is a bourgeoisie." Ryan guffawed.

"Boojie Tennis Wiley." Brian Marshall declared grinning from ear to ear. "Mr. Boojie Wiley."

Normally, he wouldn't care. They could think what they wanted and call him whatever their little minds wanted, but Jordan had been there watching them as they teased him.

At least he had not joined in with the rest of the boys who were calling him Boojie Wiley. Jordan's friends hadn't participated either. The one named Shawn looked like he had wanted to but Jordan had said something to him, and he too had stayed in his corner biting his lips as if he was barely holding himself back.

The others teased him through the recess period quite forgetting that previously they were at each other's throats about whose favorite artiste was better. He had become a common enemy.

They were probably waiting for him to start crying so that they could tease him some more but he would never give them the satisfaction.

People ridiculed what they couldn't understand. He knew

that. He was a little bit more mature than they were. Their ridicule could not last forever. He weathered it until the next class began and they had something else to focus on.

It was quite a week at his new school.

He watched as the rain started a steady drizzle on the windshield and sighed. He wondered if it was feasible to switch high schools at this juncture.

"That's a huge sigh." His mother looked at him with concern. "You sure you okay?"

He shook his head. She wouldn't understand. She would probably go to his head teacher and complain and make it worse for him if he told her about being teased.

He looked through the window and then straightened up in his seat when he saw Jordan and his friends joking with each other as they headed to the town area.

They didn't care about the impending rain or the fact that they were on the verge of getting wet. They were preoccupied with some conversation or the other…having what looked to him like a whale of a time.

The one called Shawn was demonstrating something to the rest of the boys, and they were cracking up with laughter.

His chest felt heavy, and he felt as if he had difficulty breathing as he watched them.

He knew what was wrong with him. He envied them. They were normal boys having fun.

He was never going to fit in if his mother picked him up from school in her BMW every day. Nor would he ever shake the nickname Boojie if he didn't at least attempt to find common ground with the boys his age.

He had the tastes of a middle-aged woman. It sounded bad, but it was true. He liked the things his mother liked because that was all he had ever known. He had no other choice.

He glanced at his mother, and she smiled at him.

"You'll do fine. Trust me. Everybody has issues settling in at high school. I hated my first couple of weeks too. Well, I might have hated my whole high school experience, but that's another story. You are different. You are a boy... a handsome boy. There is no way you will remain unpopular for long."

Preston grunted.

He would remain unpopular, looks or not, if he didn't have many things in common with his peers.

He didn't want to be like his mother, no way. He already made a terrible blunder echoing her thoughts on his first day of school.

It was no secret that she had always wanted a girl. Instead, she got him and then Walter and then Saint. All boys. His father always said that she cuddled them too much.

He didn't think anybody got it as bad as he did though.

He was the first-born. His mother's sounding board. He knew way too much about females at his age. He knew way too much about her life and her bitterness at his age.

He was beginning to resent it.

His mother turned up the hill and avoided the traffic in the town and headed toward Bonnie View where Walter and Saint's school was. It was his beloved old school. He wished that they had a high school section.

"That boy." His mother glanced at him. "I saw you looking at him earlier. You ever speak to him?"

"Which boy?" Preston frowned.

"Jordan, I think his name is..." Jennifer gritted her teeth as if it genuinely hurt her to say his name.

"We are in the same class," Preston said reluctantly.

Jennifer swallowed. "Same class? Why didn't you tell me? I could have gotten it sorted out!"

"It is fine, Mom." Preston looked at his mother quizzically.

Why was she so afraid of him being in contact with Jordan? It must have crossed her mind that it would happen some time or the other. Portland was a small parish. They lived less than five minutes from each other in the same district of Drapers. They were the same age.

"It is not fine." Jennifer hissed, "Not fine. Do not become friends with that boy."

"But why?" Preston asked, genuinely puzzled. He had always accepted the fact that the mere mention of the other Wiley's got his mother in an agitated state but seeing Jordan these past couple of days; he was questioning what was so bad about him. He had not teased him today.

He could have, but he didn't. He had not even allowed his friends to participate. That accounted for something.

"He is an abomination… a terrible curse from God," Jennifer said feverishly. "His mother is an evil witch, and we will not accept his existence!"

Preston subsided in his seat. "Okay."

He knew better than to argue, especially when his mother's veins bunched up at the side of her head and she had that battle light in her eye, and she started getting ecclesiastical.

Next, he was going to hear about them burning in hell with the wicked because they were illegitimate spawns of the devil. It was becoming tiring.

Jennifer exhaled in a huff. "If you really want to change schools I could get you into Portland High, my old school. It is a private school."

"No thanks," Preston said dully. "As you said it takes a while to adjust."

"Does that boy have anything to do with how you feel?" Jennifer asked suspiciously.

"No." Preston shook his head, "it's the other boys in the class. They tease me and call me Boojie."

Jennifer smiled. "That's not exactly a bad thing. At least they know that you are not the same as they are."

"But I don't want to be different." Preston insisted knowing that it was a losing battle trying to appeal to his mom. "I want to be a normal student."

"Being one of the masses is so unappealing," Jennifer snorted. "Be happy that you are a privileged young man. They tease you because they wish they were you."

"I don't think so." Preston frowned. "They tease me because I am weird. Mom, I think I want to find my way home after school."

Jennifer turned into the parking lot of Bonnie View Prep and stopped the car. "Preston, you are just twelve years old..."

Preston held himself tensely waiting for the rest of her excuses not to give him his freedom.

Walter and Saint clamored into the car, while his mother tried to formulate her reasons for not allowing him to be a regular boy.

"How are my babies?" She looked at Walter and Saint. "And how was orientation?"

"I am not a baby, Mom," Walter said frowning. "I am ten."

He was highly resistant to motherly cuddling, and Preston admired him for it. He figured if Walter demanded to take the bus, no excuse from his mother could stop him. She would just show up at the prep school, and Walter wouldn't be around.

Walter had an independent, stubborn streak that his mother had trouble taming.

"Okay then, my only baby Saint. How are you?"

"I am good, Mommy," Saint said smiling.

He really did look saintly, Preston thought resentfully. Saint had perfected the art of looking innocent while getting into trouble and had that cuteness about him that was hard to resist. He had big green eyes and light brown curls, and he looked more like the Riddley side of the family than the Wiley's.

Jennifer went off into her how-was-school-today speech, and he had to sit down and listen as one by one Walter and then Saint recounted their day. It was orientation week; usually, school ended at three, a good two hours after his school ended. It would be much easier for his mother to only collect the younger boys and leave him to find his way home. It would be easier and less time consuming for her to just pick up his brothers than to make two trips.

She had deliberately forgotten his request to let him take the bus, Preston thought resentfully, or she was just ignoring it.

They stopped at Wiley Groceries, the largest supermarket in Port Antonio. It was also the most thoroughly stocked and cleanest place to shop. It was slightly on the outskirts of town with a large parking lot.

This was the Wiley Groceries headquarters, which was conveniently on their way home.

There were two other Wiley Groceries, one was located in the busy downtown area, and one was at Annotto Bay, those were much smaller and catered to the local crowd. This big one was more touristy.

His father had taken over from grandfather Riddley and had expanded the business and their fortunes.

His mother managed the warehouse and was purchasing manager. Her office was downstairs. His father was the head of the business; his office was upstairs the supermarket itself.

His mother had something pressing to do at the office before she dropped them home. Instead of going with her to her office, Preston headed upstairs to see his father. He needed to make an appeal for his freedom. His father would make a good advocate.

****

Joseph Wiley was on the phone when he stepped into his office. The door was wide open, but he knocked politely anyway, his dad was a stickler for those kinds of mannerly things. He sat across from the desk moving a box of sample products from the chair and tried to be as quiet as he could.

It sounded like the phone conversation was with a distributor, and things were not going right. His father covered the phone and attempted a smile. It didn't quite reach his eyes. "How is it going, son?"

"I need to talk to you about something," Preston said straightening up in his seat.

Joseph nodded. "Okay, as soon as I am done with this call."

Preston looked around the office. It was as familiar to him as his room at home. He had spent many times in the corner quietly coloring while his father conducted business. He preferred it up here to his mother's office in the warehouse.

It was quieter, had more space, and his father always had him sampling stuff and giving his opinion. Those were their father/son bonding times. Their only times. He didn't get the chance to at home when his father was home.

He wondered how his father bonded with Jordan? Did they play football together? What sorts of things did they do together?

He knew that they went out together as a family. His mother would always have a mini breakdown when she heard about them.

"Why don't you take out this family to wherever it is you have to go?" His mother would rage.

"Because it would involve going with you and you won't let me go out with the boys alone." Would be his father's answer.

And then there would be howling and screaming and screeching.

He wondered if his parents realized how tense and afraid they made them feel when they interacted? Saint was sure to wet his bed after a session like that and Walter would just clam up and act like a deaf-mute for days.

He sighed and tried to drag his mind from his mixed up mad family.

There were several framed newspaper articles about Wiley Groceries and Joseph Wiley. The one he liked the best was the one with the headline: *Going From Strength to Strength the Unstoppable Joseph Wiley*. The picture underneath it was of his father and mother and him as a toddler. They were posing at this location when it was just an empty lot.

The other framed photo that he was fond of was: *Local Boy Makes A Success of His Life*. That one was old, maybe two years before he was born.

It was the closest to the desk, and Preston went over to read it while his dad carried on his never-ending conversation with whoever was on the line.

Today marks the tenth anniversary of Joseph Wiley's stunning rise up the ranks of the supermarket chain. The former warehouse assistant is now the head of the supermarket.

To hear him tell it, Gustavos Riddley his former boss, now father-in-law, saw something in him that was remarkable.

"He called me one day while I was in the warehouse unloading boxes from a delivery truck," Joseph said, "and he asked me if I wanted to do better. Of course, I said yes. I was ambitious, eager to learn and ready for whatever

opportunities he had in mind for me. At that time I was the sole breadwinner at my house, my father had just died in a boating accident..."

"Yes, Preston," his father said briskly before he could move on to the rest of the article. He knew it by heart anyway. Preston turned around and sat back in his vacated seat.

"Dad, I want to be able to take the bus home from school. I don't want mommy to pick me up anymore."

His father steepled his fingers together. "Why?"

"Jordan takes the bus," Preston said impulsively. He figured that this argument would succeed above all others. Why could Jordan do these things when they were the same age?

"Jordan takes the bus." His father repeated it and then chuckled. "You didn't say this to your mother did you?"

"No. I know how she gets. She told me not to talk to him ever." Preston shook his head. "I just want to be normal. They called me Tennis Boojie Wiley or Boojie Tennis Wiley."

"Jordan teased you?" His father asked alarmed.

"No. He didn't." Preston sighed. "He doesn't talk to me at all."

"Why do they call you Boojie?" His father grinned. "I get the tennis, it's your favorite game, but boojie?"

"As in bourgeoisie." Preston sighed. "We were looking at the working class or proletariat and the opposite class the bourgeoisie who controlled the wealth and were different from the regular people. So they started calling me boojie as short for bourgeoisie."

"Ah." His father looked at him for a long time before he sighed. "We can't have that."

"No." Preston shook his head vigorously. "I don't want to be a boojie."

"Well," his father leaned his head back in the chair and

sighed. "I guess you are old enough to take the bus home if that is what you really want."

Preston nodded eagerly. "That's what I really want."

"Your mother will take some convincing." Joseph sighed. "She considers her time with you after school to be special."

"Please help me, Dad, please," Preston pleaded. "I don't want to be the kid that stands out like a sore thumb."

"Okay." His father nodded. "I usually don't interfere when it comes to your mother's rules for you, but you are growing up. We can't have you being too boojie, can we?"

Chapter Three

Joseph was not as confident when he stepped into the house that night. Jennifer was not the easiest of persons to reason with, because of that he usually tried to keep their conversations short and infrequent.

They discussed the business, they discussed the weather, if it would impact the business, and that was that. Everything else led to an argument. Living with Jennifer was like traversing a minefield.

What they had was more of a business partnership with him being the lesser partner. They had never gotten past their initial beginning. He had steadily climbed the ranks up the supermarket ladder because of her father Gus Riddley until he became assistant purchasing manager.

Jennifer had just left university in Kingston and had been his boss. He had never liked her. She had an entitled attitude that used to grate on his last nerve.

It was shocking to him when one day she had asked him

quite aggressively if he thought she was pretty.

He had not had time to formulate a diplomatic answer. The truth was he had never really looked at her as someone other than his boss. The thought had never crossed his mind to question whether she should be desired.

He had bungled his answer. "Define pretty," he had finally stuttered.

She had looked at him so disappointed after that he had felt bad about his response.

She wasn't unattractive; through no fault of her own, she had the kind of face that looked like she was serious all the time. It was just her neutral expression like she was silently judging you.

She was very fair skinned with a long rope of hair that she always clipped back and out of her face. She was hairy, hairy arms and legs; she even had hair on her top lip and under her chin. If she slipped with shaving, it was pretty obvious. She rarely slipped though. She was very self-conscious about it.

Her eyes were big; her cheeks plump, her lips thin and always seemed to be pursed. She had an average sized body, and she dressed professionally.

She wasn't ugly. If she made an effort, she would probably have the guys in the warehouse acting giddy. But she didn't make an effort, and he just did not find her attractive.

That had been the wrong time to be asking him about her being attractive anyway. He was in love with Hannah Kennedy, always had been. They knew each other from high school, though he had been five years older than Hannah. The very moment he had seen her he had known that she was the one.

Hannah had moved in with him after she got pregnant at fifteen. And then six months in she had lost the baby. He had grown up pretty fast after that. He didn't want to be a young father with nothing to offer his children. That was when he had gotten a job as a loader on one of the biscuit delivery trucks. It was a steady wage that gave them enough to buy food.

He would show up at Riddley's supermarket every other Wednesday to unpack the truck. And old man Riddley had taken a liking to him. He went out of his way to converse with him.

He had asked him about his external passes after high school and had been surprised to hear that he got seven subjects.

That must have impressed the old man because one day out of the blue he told him that he had spoken to an administrator at the College of Agriculture Science and Education and they were waiting on his transcript.

"If they accept you, I will pay for it." Gus Riddley had looked at him challengingly. "I will pay for all your school-related expenses and your transport and give you the same money you get now packing trucks."

"What's the catch?" Joseph had asked suspiciously. Old man Riddley was not known for his generosity. He treated everybody like a potential criminal until he could prove that they were not.

"You do well and come work for me." Riddley had said, "I know potential when I see it. You got potential."

He had excelled in college and finished his Business Studies degree in three years. Riddley was pleased; his father Walter Case Wiley was even more pleased. He was the only one from his family to graduate from college.

His father was a fisherman; his father's father was a fisherman. That's all they did, lived off the sea. He had broken the family mold.

And then a few months after his twenty-fourth birthday,

while working at the supermarket as assistant to Jennifer in the warehouse, his father died unexpectedly in a boating accident.

He was heartbroken. And he believed that this was where it all went downhill for him.

After his father's death, he found out that his house that they were living in was mortgaged to the hilt. He had mere weeks to find alternative accommodation for him and Hannah because he could not afford to pay off the mortgage.

And then Gus Riddley had called him into his office, lit a cigarette and then told him that he was dying from lung cancer.

Joseph had looked from him to the cigarette and watched as he took a long inhale and then cough.

"How long do you have?" He had asked pointedly.

Gus had laughed. "The doctors say three months. I think I want to go out with a bang. Not a whimper. So I smoke, I drink, I make love to loose women."

Gus had looked at Joseph through the cigarette smoke. "I want you to head this place. I groomed you for it. Jenny endorses it wholeheartedly. I have the papers drawn up. Sixty- Forty.

"Sixty for Jenny, she is my only child and forty for you but..." he had drawn another smoke-filled breath and seemed to savor it. "Only if you marry her. Jenny says she loves you."

"But, I don't love her!" Joseph had protested. *I don't even like her.* But of course, he couldn't say that to the old man. "I already have a girlfriend. I want to marry her soon."

"It doesn't matter." Gus Riddley had pointed at him with one nicotine-stained finger, "You are a shrewd man. You know the advantages here. I'll pay your father's mortgage; your girlfriend will have a place to stay.

"Think about the benefits of marrying Jenny. You get to live in a mansion with a view; you share profit in a very profitable business. You take care of this business like it's your own and your children with Jenny will inherit a moneymaker. Jenny will get her heart's desire."

"I can't do it." Joseph had not even been swayed. He didn't care what Jennifer Riddley wanted.

"Your girlfriend, Hannah." Joseph had leaned forward and looked at him with watering eyes. "She is a beauty. I've seen her. How long do you think she will stick around with you when you are homeless and jobless?"

"Huh?" Joseph had looked into Gus' shrewd eyes.

"If you don't marry my daughter. I'll fire you. You will lose that house. I will blackball you to all the businesses in this town. I will make sure you have nowhere to rent. We are a small town, Joseph, and most people owe me money."

He had taken the deal. How could he not? Gus Riddley was not someone to be taken lightly.

They had married two months before Gus Riddley died; it was an elaborate ceremony with all the bigwigs in the parish attending. They were featured in the local papers. The stylists and makeup artists had transformed Jennifer into a fairytale princess look alike, and he had played the part of prince charming.

The pictures were pretty, but it was the most miserable day of his life up to that point.

Hannah had left him and Portland, and he had no idea where she had gone.

He had spent his wedding night with Jennifer, resenting her. He couldn't bear to look at her, much less to think about sex.

But they had consummated their marriage six months later. He had been three sheets to the wind drunk and he usually never drank.

That was thirteen years ago.

He could count on his fingers the number of times he slept with his wife. She usually came to his bed when she wanted a child when she was at her most fertile, and he had resentfully done his duty.

That arrangement had resulted in three boys.

And Jennifer had made it clear to him that they were hers. He was just a sperm donor. She also made it clear that they were not to be contaminated with his other life. The life he had with Hannah.

Just as he had made it clear that without Hannah he couldn't live with her.

When Hannah returned to Portland almost a year after his marriage, to Jennifer, they had picked up where they had left off.

And so they had an understanding, the three of them, even though Jennifer liked to pretend that she was above the fray and she was not aware of the status quo.

He dutifully worked at the supermarket, because he loved the business and wanted to see it succeed. It was a personal milestone for him to make it better than how Gus Riddley left it.

Most of his salary went to Hannah and the children he had with her. His partnership money went into a secret account for when he inevitably had to leave. He played devoted husband in public to Jennifer. He spent his weeknights at the mansion in his suite, but he never integrated himself into Jennifer's household.

The weekends, holidays and any day offs, he spent with Hannah and his boys.

Six sons later, he wasn't sure that this was the best arrangement for all of them.

He needed to follow his heart and do what he wanted for once. Thirteen years was a long time to play the martyr. Jennifer did not make him happy. The mansion on the hill with a view did not make him happy. He hardly spent time here anyway. When he was with Hannah and his boys on Spring Street in Drapers in their modest accommodation, there, he was the man of the house, he had a say in his sons' upbringing. He could play with them, laugh with them and tell stories of his youth. He could be himself.

He didn't have to take deep breaths and psyche himself up over a simple matter as this. Preston wanted to take the bus, that was more than reasonable, except in Jennifer's world.

He found her in the kitchen. The place was fancy, built to cater for an army. Everything in it was state-of-the-art. In the thirteen years since he had resided at the house, he had never taken the time to prepare a meal in the kitchen; it was so alien to him. Jennifer had never tasted his cooking. She probably didn't even know that he loved to cook.

"Hey," he said softly; he didn't want to spook her.

She spun around. She was in wide-legged pants that looked like a skirt and a floral peasant blouse that downplayed her generous bosom.

Her hair was out and down her back and around her shoulders in a soft cloud. She looked approachable, softer.

"Hello, Joseph." Jennifer smiled at him pleasantly. "How are you?"

So, she was in a light mood. Good. Joseph walked further into the kitchen and sat on one of the bar stools.

"Preston begged me to ask you to allow him to take the bus home from school."

"Hmmm." Jennifer cupped her chin in her hand and sighed. "I am not unreasonable I was thinking about it. I wasn't ready for him to be a latchkey kid. So I came up with this solution.

My cousin Glenda has a friend who is migrating to Cayman, and her helper will be free. Glenda desperately wanted her, but I need her more. We haven't had a permanent helper in two years."

Joseph bit his lip. They couldn't keep a helper because of Jennifer's erratic behavior. The poor helpers were harangued until they quit. The last one had left in the rain, without her things.

She had sworn never to come back. He was the one who had packed up her belongings from the pool house and returned them to her.

"This helper checks out well. Glenda says she is a saint because her previous employers treated her terribly. She's a widow. Her husband was a policeman who was killed in the line of duty, and she is young enough to manage the workload here. She is just forty-five."

Joseph declined to comment. Jennifer had a mean streak; this lady would have to be a saint to work with her.

"The only problem with her is that she has a kid. A girl who is a year younger than Preston, which would make her a year older than Walter. I don't want an alien influence on my sons."

Joseph nodded politely. His input was not welcomed or required. Jennifer made all hiring decisions for the house.

"The truth is, nobody in Portland will work here," Jennifer said ruefully, "and I cannot keep hiring and firing workers to clean this mammoth house. I need a full-time helper."

Joseph nodded again.

"So I guess Pamela Stone will have to do." Jennifer sighed. "When she is here full time then Preston can take the bus. At least, someone will be here when he gets home."

"Sounds good." Joseph yawned and got up. "He'll be happy about that."

"I was thinking though, that I should move him from that school."

Joseph slumped his shoulders. "Why?"

"Because there is another Wiley in his class." Jennifer hissed. The lighthearted Jennifer was gone.

He could feel a fight coming on.

"If you are petty enough to take your son from one of the best high schools because you do not want him to interact with his brother you are crazier than I thought."

"That boy is not his brother." Jennifer huffed. "He is a result of an extramarital relationship that you have hung over my head for years because you want me to suffer. Hannah Kennedy and her children are your beating stick. Your proverbial middle finger to our marriage."

Joseph curled his hand into a fist and counted to ten.

"I know I am not desirable or attractive," Jennifer was warming up, "I know I was not your first choice or any choice for that matter, but you could have some respect and stop flaunting your relationship with Hannah for the whole community to see."

"How do I do that?" Joseph asked calmly.

"Just last week you took her and her brats to the jerk festival in Boston."

Joseph leaned on the wall and put his hand in his pocket. He had never done anything as a family with Jennifer and the boys. The thought had never occurred to him because in his mind they were not a family. Maybe that was why she was looking at him with such venom in her eyes.

"Boston is ten miles from here. It is not exactly the immediate community. I am careful to separate my life with them from the one that you and I have."

"It is not enough!" Jennifer screeched, "You need to leave her. It is entirely her fault that we live like this. I am your wife! I am supposed to be the special one. I am the reason why you can comfortably live the way you do. I convinced my father to take you out of your poverty and the filth you were coming from. You should worship the very ground I walk on; instead, you flaunt her in front of me! You ungrateful user!"

Joseph watched as she worked herself up into a froth.

He deserved this.

He shouldn't have gotten married to Jennifer. He had sold himself, and now they were both trapped.

"I'll leave," he said quietly. "I should have done so a long time ago."

"Over your dead body." Jennifer snarled. "Till death do us part, Mister. You will never be free of me so that you can be with her. Oh no, if I am to suffer in this prison of a marriage so will you."

Joseph inhaled deeply and then closed his eyes. He was too tired for this.

"I can't chain you up and keep you here." Jennifer snarled, "but I am telling you now. Not one dime from my father's legacy will be spent on that woman or her brats.

"The cars, the house, the business, all mine. I hope your little hussy knows that if you divorce me, your token forty percent of the company stays with me. If you die, it stays with me. How does she feel to know that you love money and a place as token head of my father's business more than you love her?"

Joseph cracked his mouth open but didn't respond. He had heard this before. She was just getting warm.

"I own you." Jennifer roared, "I am the reason your little brat can even go to high school. If he says anything to my precious son, I'll get him kicked out. It would be my pleasure if they would just die. All of them. And vanish off the face of this earth!"

"Mom!" Preston's voice intruded on the gathering rage in Joseph's chest.

Preston had heard all of it. He was standing at the door his eyes wide and shiny with tears.

This was not the first time Jennifer wished death on Hannah's sons. The first time Joseph heard her say this, Jordan was just a baby. He had only barely restrained himself from hitting her then. She drove him into an unspeakable rage when she spoke like this.

Jennifer looked at the door, her face stricken. She usually tried to pretend to be the perfect mother. Preston had just gotten an earful and an eyeful of just how unhinged his mother was. *Poor kid.*

Joseph exhaled and pushed himself from the wall. He didn't even look at his wife or his son as he headed for his quarters.

This was his last year as Jennifer's whipping boy. His partnership money from the supermarket was beckoning. He had been saving it religiously for the past nine years in an account with Hannah, just four more years and it would mature into a very healthy balance. It was their escape money. They could probably open another supermarket with it.

It was getting closer to the time when he would make a move. He would take Hannah and his sons out of Portland and not look back. Enough was enough.

Chapter Four

"**F**amily tree homework," Jordan said slapping down his knapsack on his mother's salon center table with her girly magazines. She was in the middle of washing a customer's hair.

"What happened to basic manners?" Hannah looked over at him and frowned.

"Good evening mommy and miss... er..." Jordan said hurriedly. "Sorry."

"Miss Violet," Hannah said helpfully.

"And good evening Aunt Jackie," Jordan said when Jackie came from the back with a stack of freshly washed towels in her hands.

"Good evening child," Miss Violet said. His mother helped her up from her bent over position and started applying something to her hair.

"Hi Jordy," Jackie grinned at him. "Where is Shawn?"

"She stopped at home to change clothes and do her

homework."

"Good," Jackie grunted. "I threatened to stop her from coming here if she doesn't do her homework.."

"That's very effective Jackie." Miss Violet grinned." I can understand why your girl will be so drawn to this boy; he is very handsome."

Miss Violet turned to Jordan. "When you grow up, you should marry my daughter, Lynette. She is fourteen now, but in a couple of years it won't matter."

Jackie laughed.

"I will come back when you are not busy, mommy," Jordan said backing out of the room.

"Take your bag with you." Hannah chuckled. "I'll be over soon."

Jordan grabbed his bag and went to the connecting door to where the living quarters were.

Today was supposed to be his mother's day off. Miss Violet was probably an emergency customer.

His mother had only recently started doing the hairdressing business full time with Jackie as her partner. She had converted the side of the house into a beauty parlor. Previously it was rented to tenants.

It had a bedroom, which was now a shampoo area, a bathroom, a largish living room, which was now both reception area, and where they styled and did all sorts of hair related stuff. It also had a small enclosed back veranda.

It had become a thriving business. Already they had two full-time assistants and somebody that did nails exclusively.

These days, he hardly entered the main house through the parlor, because the place was usually filled with women who cooed over how handsome he was and how they wanted him to marry their daughters.

It was crazy talk.

He entered their living room and saw Guy lying on the floor reading. Not a book with color and pictures but what looked like one of his English Literature books. Guy was the weirdest nine-year-old boy on the planet.

He much preferred reading to playing, and he probably had a much better vocabulary than he did.

"What are you reading, Guy?" Jordan asked.

"Your book, A Cow Called Boy," Guy looked up at him, "very interesting."

"I haven't read it yet." Jordan frowned. "I am going to change my clothes and meet Shawn by her house; you should come too. We could play cricket."

Guy looked torn. He wanted to hang out with his big brother, but he also loved the book.

Hanging out with Jordan won over reading, and he nodded. "Are you two going to allow me to bat today?"

"Sure!" Jordan nodded. "Where's Case?"

He looked around the living room for his baby brother, sometimes Case did an impromptu hide and seek because he wanted you to find him.

It was kind of ridiculous since the house had a simple layout, nobody could get lost in it. The house had a large living room—a half-wall separated the settees, television, and bookcase from the dining room. Beyond that was the kitchen.

His mother's room was off to one side of the house. It had an en-suite bathroom. A smaller room was also on that side of the house, but his mother used it as storage. He had his own room, and he shared a bathroom with his brothers who both shared a room.

"Case is at Aunty Monique's," Guy said. "I would have stayed with her, but I wanted to come home to read."

"Okay." Jordan headed to his bedroom.

Aunt Monique was his mother's eldest sister. She was a grade five teacher at the primary school that Guy and Case currently attended. His old school.

The boys would go home with her after school because she lived close to the school on a mini farm. It was a child's paradise. The farm had numerous fruit trees to climb and raid, a yard that was big enough to play in, and four dogs, two cats and three rabbits and a stream where they could fish if they had a mind to.

Jordan contemplated going there now instead of hanging out at Shawn's place. He pulled on his jeans shorts, a t-shirt, and a cap. It might rain. Or he might need the cap to carry guavas or plums. Most of the trees were loaded with those fruits now.

Just then, he heard his father's voice in the living room—and Guy's excited voice as well. He ran out of the room in a hurry.

His dad rarely showed up at the house at this time of the day, especially not on a Tuesday. Unless he was dropping off a treat or heading up to San San where he had property. They loved to go up there with him. It was better than any adventure at Aunt Monique's. He was almost sure that they had not explored half of the land up there yet.

"Dad!" Jordan squealed when he saw his father, who was dressed in jeans, hiking boots, and a polo shirt.

If his dressing was any indication, they were going to be in for an adventure.

"Jordan!" His father grinned with him. "Go put on your boots, both of you. And carry Case's, we have business to attend to."

Jordan couldn't stop grinning from ear to ear. "Can we bring Shawn too?"

"Sure." Joseph shook his head. "Shawn is my defacto son,

daughter or whatever it is she is these days.”

“And carry a bag, several bags.” Joseph added, “I know there are loads of fruits probably begging to be picked up there.”

Jordan and Guy argued about who should ride shotgun in their father’s Jeep. Heads or tails solved it for them. Guy won, he called head. They stopped to pick up Shawn who was just as excited as they were for the trip.

Drapers was just fifteen minutes from where they were going to San San, but it was still an adventure. His father’s property was very close to Frenchman’s Cove—a very popular tourist spot. And they had the same kind of views, except their place was wild and unexplored and looked forest-like from the road.

They stopped on the way for Case who was almost delirious with happiness when he saw that it was his dad who was coming to get him.

“Okay sons and Shawn.” Joseph stopped at the boundary of his twelve-acre property and parked the jeep. “This is what is called prime real estate.”

“Prime!” Jordan repeated dutifully.

“We have an unfettered sea view, fruited trees, and a river that runs through a piece of the property.”

“My piece,” Guy said possessively. “I want to farm my piece so I’ll need water. I want to be a farmer.”

Joseph chuckled. “My son knows what he wants to be at nine. Farming is not a bad choice, Guy.”

They slowly walked on the outskirts of the property. “I could sell this for many millions of dollars.” Joseph continued, “but I won’t. My father left it for me, and I am going to leave it to my six sons. Two acres for each boy. Today, I had that put in writing. If I have other children, then I’ll just have to find more land.”

"I hope you don't end up living beside Boojie Wiley," Shawn whispered to Jordan when his father was out of earshot.

"Stop calling him that." Jordan pinched her. "He is taking the bus now. Didn't you see him?"

"I saw him." Shawn grimaced. "He looked like he was going to piss himself today. I don't know why you insisted on us making sure that he was okay to go to the bus stop."

"Because he is my brother." Jordan shrugged. "There is something about him that I like. He may be older by a couple of weeks, but he is so helpless when it comes to the real world."

Shawn rolled her eyes. "You like him because you like your own face. You are so vain."

"And you are a girl," Jordan said sticking his tongue out at her.

"That's the best insult you can come up with?" Shawn poked him in the side.

"For you it is an insult." Jordan poked her back.

"Cut it out." Joseph looked behind at them and then frowned at Jordan, "and don't be pushing and shoving Shawn; she is a girl. Girls are delicate creatures that should be handled with care."

"Okay, now I am insulted," Shawn muttered and then gave Jordan a hard shove that had him almost landing on his face.

****

The name Boojie had stuck. It wasn't going away. By October Preston was learning to live with it. He hadn't exactly started to like school yet, but he was tolerating it. They left him alone for the most part, mainly because he started to take his break times away from the classroom. As soon as school ended he headed to the bus stop and made his way home to where he had blessedly found a friend.

Miss Pamela Stone was like a breath of fresh air in his house. She was calmer than his mother, for one, and he could talk to her about Jordan without fear of her having a heart attack.

Jordan was his favorite topic of conversation with Miss Pam. The most fascinating person in his day.

He knew that Jordan and his friends walked behind him to make sure that he took the right bus home the first day. He also knew that for the past two weeks or so, they continued to trail him to the bus stop and then waited to make sure he was okay before they went off to wherever it is that they got up to.

He dearly wished that he knew what they did with their time.

That was all he speculated about the first week Miss Pam came to work with them. He and Miss Pam had gotten off to a fine start. She had one child, a girl, who still lived in Kingston with Miss Pam's mother.

Her name was Sheryl, and she was going to an all girls' school on a scholarship. To hear Miss Pam tell it, she was a genius. She had gotten into high school at ten. Much younger than he got in. And she was now in second form. She carried a picture of Sheryl in a locket around her neck.

Along with a picture of her husband who had died in the line of duty as a policeman.

"I like Portland." Miss Pam had said to him on the second day of her work there, "and I like you, Jordan. You seem like a very nice kid, your mother and father have done a good job raising you."

The compliment still had the power to make him grin, even weeks after.

He let himself into the house after getting off the bus and headed to the kitchen. Usually, at this time of the day, that was where he would find Miss Pam. She always cooked lunch for him.

She was making guava jam. He could smell it from the entrance of the house. He changed his clothes first before joining her in the kitchen.

"Your father carried a whole bag full of guavas." Miss Pam said pointing to the mound of guavas on the table. "I asked him to carry some jars to put the jam in; you folks will have homemade jam for a long, long time."

Preston nodded and licked his lips. "It depends on what you call long, jam is Walter's favorite food. He'll eat it with a spoon from the jar."

Miss Pam chuckled. "Well then, Walter will be very happy for the next couple of weeks."

Preston drew up a stool and watched her as she poured out guava jam into empty glass jars. He counted twenty-five of them.

"Maybe you can give Jordan one." Miss Pam suggested, "or give him three, for each of your other brothers."

Preston shook his head. "He'll probably think it's poison and chuck it. I have never spoken to him, and then I am suddenly giving him jam. I would find it suspicious if I were in his shoe."

Miss Pam grimaced. "You know this is unhealthy, Preston. You want to talk to him, you should. He is your brother, your own flesh and blood. You should have a relationship with him if you want. You don't even have to let your mother know." Miss Pam lowered her voice, even though they were at the house alone.

"She would know," Preston mumbled, "and she would kill me."

"She wouldn't, your mother loves you like a lioness but kill you, I doubt that."

Miss Pam folded her arms and looked at Preston contemplatively, "Normally, I would never encourage a child to disobey a parent, but in this case, I think that the parent is very unreasonable. Granted, I've only been here for a month, and I shouldn't interfere, but this situation is very unfair to you."

Preston nodded eagerly. "It is unfair."

"You know, I met Hannah yesterday."

"Jordan's mom?" Preston rounded his eyes. "I saw her once. She looks like a movie star."

Miss Pam laughed. "Yes, she is a very glamorous looking woman. She puts herself together nicely."

"How did you meet her?" Preston asked curiously.

"She was highly recommended to me by a friend of a friend who lives here in Portland. I need to get my hair done, so I visited her shop to make an appointment and see what she had to offer. I always do my research when it comes to my hair."

Preston nodded dutifully. His mother didn't go to a hairdresser. Her hair was always in the same style, pulled back and in a single plait down her back. He had no experience with hairdressers or those sorts of things. He hadn't even known that Hannah was a hairdresser. He had thought that she just sat around and looked pretty all day. Whenever he overheard his mother talking about her, she always referred to Hannah as a lazy mistress trying to get as much money as she could from his father.

"I was thinking," Miss Pam finished pouring the jam and started covering them up, "do you want to meet me there, tomorrow afternoon after school?"

"I couldn't...I can't...it would be crazy. If my mom found

out, she would probably explode. Like literally explode. And she would fire you." Preston frowned. "I like you, Miss Pam, you just got here."

"Okay," Miss Pam nodded, "have it your way."

"Don't let my mom know you are going to Hannah," Preston added seriously. "She will probably still explode."

"Ah, young man." Miss Pam grinned, "She would have to explode. If Hannah is as good with my hair as I hear she is with other people's, I have no plans to go to anyone else."

Chapter Five

Hannah slid reluctantly into the bench at the back of the Port Antonio Parish church one Sunday in early November. It was going to be a long day. A church service, which she was assured, would be blessedly short and then there would be a party, which she had stayed up most of the night helping to cater for.

All of this, because her youngest sister Sharla was having her firstborn christened. It was a huge deal for Sharla. She had almost died giving birth to Nicholas so she was determined that he would get God's full blessings.

Yesterday she had taken the baby to be blessed at Monique's church, and today the baby would be christened at the parish church.

Sharla had gone overboard and had insisted that everybody join the madhouse with her. Hannah had wanted to be a simple spectator because she had a rough week but everybody in the family had to be involved because Sharla wanted a big splash.

The Kennedy family was small. Their mother had abandoned them years ago, and their father had died shortly after.

They had just each other and a smattering of cousins who still acknowledged the connection. Monique had played the part of a mother for most of their lives. She was a few years older than both Hannah and Sharla, but she had grown them up the best that she could.

And now, they had children. Hannah had her three boys with Joseph Wiley. Monique had her triplet girls, Giselle, Tiana and Elsa with her now deceased husband, Wilton Pryce. He was an older man in his seventies, who had a heart condition.

There was no good reason for that match. Wilton hadn't even had a dime to his name except for his pension and yet Monique, lovely young Monique, married him because suddenly she was in love.

It baffled the mind. When he died a year later from a heart attack no one was particularly surprised. Wilton had not had the energy to keep up with his young wife.

People still snickered that Monique and Viagra did him in.

He left her pregnant with triplets and a lovely place to live. Though his older children were trying to take it away from her. Wilton had bought the place with his first wife and had not had the sense to make a new will.

Monique would probably be homeless soon. Her only saving grace now was that the Wilton's oldest son was a politician and needed to keep up appearances and he had some compassion for her situation.

Sharla was the only sister that did things right. Hannah thought enviously. Her husband Tanner simply adored her. He was a Canadian lawyer who had come to Jamaica last year for summer vacation, for a little fun and sun. Sharla had been his personal housekeeper at Goblin Hill Villas. By the end of the summer, they were married.

And in a couple of days, Sharla was moving to Canada to be with him. This overabundance of family celebrations was also Sharla's way of saying goodbye.

She understood it, and normally she would have no problems coming to the parish church, but this church was where Jennifer Riddley Wiley worshipped every Sunday like the dutiful society lady that she was.

Sometimes she even played the organ.

She was head of the mother's union and charity doyenne. This was Jennifer's sacred turf.

Hannah knew this, and she also knew that barring hail or storm, Sharla would be having the service right here in this church because this was where she was christened as a baby and she had to do it today in the regular service because that was the only time that the reverend could accommodate her.

"Lighten up," Monique who had taken a seat beside her whispered. "You look good, enough to make Mrs. Wiley have a heart attack if she takes her nose out of the air long enough to glance at the regular people."

Hannah giggled. Monique was always good for her self-esteem.

"You sure the children are okay?" She whispered to Monique.

"Yes." Monique nodded, "The children's church is quite lively. They will be back for the christening service."

"Okay." Hannah nodded. "I haven't been to church in a minute."

"I know," Monique wriggled her eyebrow at her, "I keep begging you to come to mine."

"You know my situation is not church friendly," Hannah

whispered. "And your church is even stricter with your requirements for membership than even this one."

Monique grunted. "You should give Joseph an ultimatum, let him leave the witch and marry you. He is more your husband than hers."

Hannah sighed and then looked around. There was no one close enough to hear Monique's criticism of her situation.

"He is working on it." Hannah glanced at her sister.

"For the past thirteen years." Monique sniffed. "Your pretty years are slowly running out while he works on it."

"I am just thirty-two," Hannah hissed, "I have pretty time left. I see some hot ladies at fifty, and beyond, I could be one of them."

Monique chuckled. "Okay, madam. I hope he comes to his senses before you hit fifty."

Hannah stared ahead while the organ was being played. She had been with Joseph for more than sixteen years. They grew up together in the same district, became intimate way too early if anyone asked. For her, it had always been him.

She was supposed to be the wife, but she wasn't, Jennifer Riddley was. The thought of it still made her uncomfortable.

Joseph had made a pragmatic decision at the time that he claimed would be best for the both of them in the long run and though she hadn't supported it, she had come around.

She would have preferred to live in poverty with him not being able to afford the basics than to have him being sold to Jennifer for thirty pieces of silver.

But she had accepted it in the long run. She had left Portland and went to Kingston and stayed with her aunt, a hairdresser who had encouraged her to get a hairdressing license. She had a knack for taking care of hair. Hers was a luscious swathe of curls that hit her a little below her waist. She took pride in it.

And then she had returned to Portland. Quite ready to move forward without Joseph in her life until he had shown up at her door. It was a Sunday like today. He was married for close to a year and so unhappy she could see it on him. He had started drinking, and he was quite literally lost.

Her heart had not melted quickly. She was hurt. She had written him off. It was time to move on.

But how did you firmly say no to the man who you had been with since fourteen, the man who was your first for everything? Whose very face made your heart contract with something akin to pain?

And when he said stuff like, *if you leave again Hannah, I am going to die. I don't want to live without you. When you are here, you make living with her bearable. I cannot go through what you put me through this past year and survive.*

What's a girl to do when he spent most of his time with her, all his vacations, all his free time? She was his family. Not Jennifer. Never Jennifer.

She opened her eyes and realized that she had not seen Jennifer today and then she spotted her way up front. She was in a light blue dress and matching pillbox hat with a little veil and white pearls at her ears and around her neck. She looked elegant. Hannah grudgingly admitted.

She must have stared too long because Jennifer turned around and looked directly at her.

No surprise to see her there. No discernible expression at all. Just a narrowing of the eyes, a tightening of the lips. Jennifer was a professional at making her displeasure known with just one look.

Hannah straightened in her seat and schooled her features into one of blankness. She did not react to the displeasure. She held Jennifer's stare. She was not going to back down from this war of wills.

Joseph had been hers first. Though this elegantly dressed woman was rich enough to buy her man, Hannah had the upper hand. She was bound to Joseph by love, not money.

It was inevitable that they would meet sometimes. It was a small town. She was never going to leave Joseph, so she just had to deal with this.

****

The party was in full swing at Monique's place when Hannah headed inside for a breather. She had no idea that Tanner's family had traveled en masse to Jamaica for the party. She had seen a few of them at the church, but now their numbers had swollen.

They were friendly.

She walked into the house when Joseph stopped her. He grabbed her around the waist and kissed her on the lips.

"Where are you going Miss Pretty?"

"To a quiet place to recharge my extrovert buttons so that I can deal with Tanner's extremely happy family." Hannah smiled at Joseph.

"Where are you going, Mr. Handsome?"

"To join a game of dominoes." Joseph swatted her on the bottom. "Love you."

"Love you too, always," Hannah whispered and watched as he walked away. Oh, she did love him. It was sometimes galling to her just how much.

Her eyes connected with Adalynn Griffith and she hurriedly looked away. Adalynn was Monique's neighbor and best friend and prayer partner and whatever. She was also a psychologist who moved to Portland five years ago and had married Pastor Tate Griffith, the pastor of Monique's church. Hannah was never comfortable around Adalynn. She always felt like she was being assessed and had fallen short.

Monique said she was being fanciful, but the truth was, the first time she had met Adalynn Griffith she was a customer in her salon. Adalynn had been in discussion with another woman, a regular customer, about an article in a magazine about women who dated married men.

Adalynn had called those women— the mistresses, abhorrent creatures who had no shame.

She had not known that Hannah was one of those abhorrent ladies who had no shame but she had found out, and since then their meetings were awkward, they didn't speak about anything personal even though Adalynn came to her parlor every other week like clockwork.

Hannah went into the hall closet and kicked off her high heels and snagged one of Monique's flats. It was a relief to be in regular shoes.

"We have never really had a personal conversation, you and I," Adalynn said behind her. "We always stick to the superficial. I know it is my fault and I want to rectify that."

Hannah spun around sharply almost losing her balance. "I didn't know you followed me inside."

Adalynn smiled. "I thought that in here was a good place to talk. We don't meet in social situations like this."

Hannah groaned inwardly. What had she done to deserve this?

"Very well," she said out loud. She walked over to the sofa and sat down.

Adalynn sat on the sofa facing her. Hannah studied her covertly. She had a thin narrow face and perfectly shaped brows. Her hair reached her chin in a thick, healthy swathe that Hannah felt professional pleasure in seeing.

"My husband tells me that you were his crush in high school." Adalynn smiled, "I never knew that you went to high school with him."

Hannah laughed. "Yes I did, Tate would send me love notes from various songs. I thought he wrote them until I heard the songs on the radio."

"I think I am jealous." Adalynn smiled.

"No need to be. If you are going to be jealous, your friend Monique is a better target." Hannah giggled. "Tate stood outside our house playing, *I Will Always Love You* country and western style on his guitar three nights straight when Monique rejected him."

Adalynn chuckled. "I have heard that story before, but he only switched his love to Monique when you got pregnant for Joseph Wiley."

"Yep. High school dropout here." Hannah winced. "Imagine, if that never happened I could be married to Tate Griffith now. First lady of Willow Tree Church."

Adalynn laughed and relaxed in the settee. "I don't suppose Tate stood a chance. With Joseph around that would never happen."

"Nah it wouldn't," Hannah said finally relaxing around Adalynn. She wasn't quoting scriptures at her or making her feel like a second-class citizen. Maybe she had misjudged her motives for wanting to have a conversation.

"You should send the boys to church with Monique. I know you don't want to come. I know Monique hounds you about attending," Adalynn said in the silence. "But I beg you, send the boys. In this world where good men are a scarcity isn't it better for them to be a part of a system that at least strives for right doing? Even though we sometimes get it wrong. At least a good percentage of us want to be Christ-like. I don't think sending your children to church will harm them. Look at the alternative, so many crazy things are happening in this world..."

Hannah sighed. "I do send them occasionally."

"I know, but I would love for it to be more consistent." Adalynn smiled. "Case was in my kindergarten class. The boy sings like an angel. You should encourage him."

"My Case?" Hannah raised her brows, "my baby can sing?"

"Yes." Adalynn nodded. "And Guy, he knows all the Bible stories accurately. You can't leave a single detail out."

Hannah smiled. "Yes, I know he is a little genius, loves to read."

"And Jordan, good heavens, he asks questions only a seasoned theologian can answer."

Hanna laughed. "Jordy is a good boy, stubborn as a donkey and very curious."

"You and Joseph produced very lovely boys. When you and Joseph decide to tie the knot, we are right here too," Adalynn said wistfully. "To have a man look at you the way he does you… I don't know how you two can stand being in this situation for so long."

Hannah bit her lip. This was something she was not willing to comment on with Adalynn. She was and would always be sensitive about this topic.

"Anyway," Adalynn smiled reading her body language perfectly and knew that it was time to move on, "I will always be here if you need to talk."

"For free or professionally?" Hannah raised an eyebrow.

"Both." Adalynn grinned, "or we could barter. You provide a service that is vital to my well-being. I can return the favor."

Hannah laughed. "We'll see about the counseling thing, but I am okay for now."

Chapter Six

Jennifer paced the house for most of the Sunday night. She could not fall asleep, though she had taken more than half the bottle of melatonin that her naturopathic doctor friend had prescribed for her insomnia.

She had cried and paced for most of the night in the master bedroom and then she had taken it outside in the garden. A heavy shower of rain greeted her as she stood on the brick walkway that led to the pool house.

She welcomed it. She did not mind the fact that the water soaked through her housecoat and her nightgown and that the rain felt like icy fingers as it battered her uncovered head.

The boys could not see her from this side of the house. She was practically alone; Miss Pam was probably fast asleep in her bed. Even if she weren't, she would not hear a thing.

She sat in the walkway and howled. Like a broken hearted dog locked up in a cage that wanted to go free.

Seeing Hannah Kennedy and her sons always did this

to her. It was not something that she could control, this bitterness that roiled through her like quicksilver. Crying seemed to make it better, shrunk it a bit, made it manageable.

She had smiled all evening while she was with her sons, spending the usually peaceful Sunday listening to them. But after they had gone to bed she had developed more cracks in her composure than a hard plastic bottle that was exposed to prolonged heat.

One day she would completely shatter or melt.

She hung her head on her shoulders because it felt too heavy for her neck.

Hannah Kennedy, how she hated the woman. She was beautiful, with skin like dark velvet, not a blemish in sight, she did not need makeup. She had natural red lips and masses of perfect curly spirally hair and a shape that caused accidents in downtown Port Antonio—men stopped to stare at her like mesmerized fools while she walked.

She couldn't have chosen a worse nemesis. The one woman who made her feel inferior without trying as if she didn't already have several hang-ups about her own looks. To make matters worse, her husband, Joseph Wiley, the man she had chosen to bail her out of spinsterhood, loved Hannah the physically perfect woman.

He adored her. He loved her. He spent his weekends with her. He was probably with her now in her bed cuddled up as they listened to the rain together. Sometimes like now when she was at her most vulnerable and raw she thought of getting her shotgun, driving over to the house on Spring Street and killing them both.

"I hate her!" Jennifer screamed. "I hate her! I hate her!"

And then she sobbed like the heartbroken reject she was, the woman who had so little self-esteem that she had to cajole her father to get Joseph Wiley to marry her—a man who was clearly not interested in her.

She had known he had a girlfriend. She had known he lived with her. She had known that his father had died and left a mortgage on the house and that Joseph was struggling to repay it. She knew that he had been in a financial bind and she had pounced.

She had wanted Joseph from the minute she had seen him unpacking the biscuit truck in the warehouse. He was handsome and polite, and she had quite literally lusted after him. She had groomed him just for her, convincing her father to invest in him. She had been the brain behind the Joseph Wiley makeover.

She didn't care how she got him. She molded him into what she wanted.

Her reasoning at the time was that she had much more to offer than Hannah who had no job and no livelihood. She had thought that Joseph would have found her at least likable.

She had coveted him. He was handsome and sweet, and she had never been kissed and had never been desired by anyone.

She wanted him to show her all the things she was missing.

Joseph had never professed to love her. She doubted he even liked her.

He had to be drunk to have sex with her. She was wasting her time holding out for some miraculous turnaround.

She was wasting her time living like this, but she didn't know how to do anything else. What was worse, she didn't want to live without him.

She loved him. She loved him as much as she hated Hannah.

A sob escaped her throat. God help her, she wasn't going to give him up.

"Mom!" Preston was at the back door in his teddy bear

pajamas looking out at her, worry creasing his little face.

His face that looked so much like his father's. At least he was all hers. Nobody else's. Especially not Joseph who had not wanted children with her.

Her sons were the only men in her life who loved her unconditionally. If she lost their love, she had no idea what she would do. Jennifer pulled herself up from the wet pavement and stumbled toward the back door.

"Preston promise you'll always love me. Only me. You have to promise."

Preston looked at her with wide, fearful eyes. "Mom, are you okay?"

"Promise me." Jennifer rasped. "Now, this minute, that you'll always love your mommy, that you will always," her voice caught on a sob, "love me no matter what."

Preston nodded. "I promise, Mommy."

Jennifer inhaled raggedly. The poor child looked scared. What kind of mother was she to be scaring him like this?

"What are you doing up?" She rubbed her eyes and willed her voice to sound normal.

"I came for some water for Saint. He was crying. I saw you through the window. You were shouting I hate her!"

"Goodness." Jennifer inhaled, "I wish you hadn't seen that. We won't speak of it again. Go upstairs. I'll bring the water for Saint."

****

"Where are you spending your Christmas, Boojie Wiley?" It was Ryan again; the boy would not leave him alone. He was endlessly curious about his business.

Preston considered telling him to mind his own business,

but he didn't. It was close to the end of school anyway. Besides, he was feeling sleepy because it was early December and the day was unusually cool.

His parents were at it again. Since the beginning of November when he had found his mother outside the house looking like a drowned rat, the house was a war zone.

His father was leaving. He had given his mother notice. He was leaving the business and them.

His mother stopped crying at the beginning of November, by mid-November she had taken up howling and shrieking. She had deep black circles under her eyes, and she had completely trashed the living room and her bedroom, and her voice was gone. She had yelled and carried on so bad she must have damaged her vocal chords.

He felt afraid.

His world was uncertain. His brothers were even more shaken up than he was, Saint had started wetting his bed again, Walter had clammed up. The boy didn't speak, no matter the prompting.

One of Walter's teachers had visited the house yesterday and had asked him what was going on.

He told her the truth—they were living in hell.

Miss Pam tried to take them out of the house for a respite, but his mother was having none of it. She wanted her babies close, to suffer through her heartbreak with her.

Nobody was telling them anything, which added to the uncertainty. Everything he knew he heard through their arguments and most of it was his mother calling his father names.

"I own you. You should worship the ground I walk on. I am the one who sent you to school and allowed you to work in my business. You are nothing without me!"

That was the last line he heard just this morning. His father had not said a word while he loaded his belongings into the jeep piece by piece.

Every time he came back into the house it was with a lighter step as if he was finally shedding a heavyweight.

Miss Pam had taken to whispering under her breath. "I now see why he has to leave. Who can stay with this kind of abuse?"

Miss Pam didn't know that he had overheard her muttering.

Ryan came into his face jolting him from his worrisome reflections. "I asked you a question Boojie? Where are you spending your Christmas? Or are you too boojie to tell me."

"Get out of my face." He was suddenly filled with anger and resentment. Leave me alone!"

"Fight!" One girl squealed. "Fight!"

He pushed back his chair, knocking over his desk, a red haze around his eye. Ryan's face was close by, and he could feel the hatred running through his blood. He wanted to crush it.

He no longer cared about his reputation or staying in school or any of that. He was going to pummel this boy to the ground to make him stop. He had had it.

He pulled back his hand to make a swing at him and instead found that he couldn't. Two persons had pinned him down.

"Leave him alone Ryan!" He heard Jordan's voice above his head. "Pretend as if he doesn't exist and stop pestering him with your questions. Why are you so curious about him, he is not a girl?"

He heard snickers as the rest of the class that had gathered like a dark cloud on a rainy day surrounded them to see the aborted fight.

"Nothing to see here." Jordan's voice again. "Preston Wiley is not interested in fights or in answering any more questions about anything regarding his life if he doesn't want to."

Ryan moved away but not without a parting shot. "I don't know why you are defending him, Jordan. He is stuck up and acts as if he is better than everybody else."

The hands holding him down loosened. He shrugged out of them and glanced behind him. It was Shawn and Cody, Jordan's closest friends.

Shawn smirked at him. "So you do have emotion. I was wondering when someone would tip you over the edge. You shouldn't hold it all in, you should let it out now and again, or this will happen."

"If you want, we could have taken him after school… beat him up for you," Cody said eagerly," or just allow you to beat him up yourself. You look like you could use a good punching session."

"And then we could get in a lick or two," Shawn was almost salivating at the thought.

"No," Jordan said gruffly, "we are not thugs."

He looked at Preston directly. It felt strange to stare into eyes that were so weirdly familiar, Jordan held his gaze.

"You okay?"

Preston nodded. His throat had suddenly closed up. He felt the insane need to cry. What was wrong with him?

"Cody's uncle has a boxing gym in town. We go there most evenings. If you want to come one evening, Derrick can give you some lessons."

"Thanks," Preston whispered, his voice choking up.

So, that's where they went off to after they saw him to the bus stop?

"I'll check with my...our dad."

Jordan smiled and nodded. "Okay. He hangs out there sometimes with us."

Chapter Seven

"Preston looks unhappy," Jordan said to his mother over their dinner. They were alone around the dining table. "I had to stop him from fighting today."

Hannah sighed. "I really feel it for Preston and his brother's, they have a very troubled mother, and they have to live with her."

"And Dad is now going to live with us full time?" Jordan pointed at the piles of suitcases and boxes in the passageway that had not yet made it into the storage room.

"Yes," Hannah smiled, "as he should be from the very beginning. We were his family first."

"But it is affecting them." Jordan pointed out. "They are his kids too."

"I know." Hannah huffed. "It's a screwed up situation, but they had him for awhile. Now it is our turn. It's only fair."

Hannah pushed away from the table and started clearing it. He could hear his brother's outside as they helped his father replace the jeep seat. He was happy that his dad was here with them and yet he was feeling a little bit sorry for the family that he left behind, which was nuts. As his mother said, they had him for a while.

It was too much for him to contemplate. He shouldn't care so much but there was something about Preston today—the boy looked like he was on the verge of a breakdown. He got up from the table and helped his mother with the dishes.

He decided to rinse while she washed. She looked across at him and smiled. "You are a good boy, Jordan."

"Huh?" Jordan looked at her quizzically.

"I tried not to think about how your dad's leaving would do to them. I..." Hannah sighed. "You are a much better person than me. I guess I should be a little less selfish. They are his children too."

She didn't say anything else until she started cleaning the stovetop. "I love your father. You know that right?"

Jordan nodded.

"This whole situation with him marrying Jennifer and having children with the both of us...it should not have happened. At least not the way it happened. I know you are too young to get this, but when you grow up, I don't want you to make such a mess of your life. Marry only for love and never have two families at once. It is more stress than its worth, and somebody will always end up getting hurt."

Jordan shrugged. "I am never marrying."

"You will." His mother grinned. "Shawn will be your bride, that's how Jackie and I planned it when you were born. I had a boy. She had a girl..."

"Eww, double eww, triple eww." Jordan shuddered.

Hannah laughed. "You say eww now that you are twelve, but you will not be saying that in a couple of years. When that girl decides to be a girl again, she will be a knockout.

You will be running to me for counsel."

"I am going to help Dad," Jordan snorted. "This is enough adult conversation for me."

Except it wasn't the end of adult conversations. His father commissioned him and Guy to help him pack his stuff in the storeroom. Case was sent off for a bath, and it was apparently man-to-man time.

His father sat on a chair in the room and pointed out his high school box. "There is my box. Open it."

Jordan opened the box and found yearbooks, pictures, a class ring and a hat with the Titchfield school logo. The box also had his dad's old khaki shirt. It had signatures all over it.

Guy grabbed the ring before he could and jammed it on his thumb. It was of course too big for him.

"Give it to Jordan, Guy." His father laughed, "Your time will come in three years."

Guy reluctantly handed Jordan the ring, picked up an old reading book and became lost in its pages.

Joseph laughed. "He will be far ahead of his peers when he is in high school."

"That's for sure." Jordan shook his head. "He has read off all my books already for this term."

"Guy," Joseph said gently, "can you give me and Jordan some time to talk privately?"

"Sure, Dad." Guy got up taking his book with him; he had already zoned them out anyway.

"Okay, good, we are alone." Joseph steepled his fingers in front of him and looked at his son. "What's happening with Preston? I overheard you telling your mom that he almost fought today."

"Yes." Jordan nodded.

Joseph sighed after Jordan told him what happened.

"I wish I could undo this."

"You would go back to live with them?" Jordan furrowed his brow.

"No." Joseph shook his head. "I would go back and have a different relationship with my sons…with Jennifer. I love them. They are mine too. I gave up on being a father to them because that is what she wanted. I shouldn't have done what she wanted."

Jordan nodded.

"You remember the talk that you and I had before school began?" Joseph looked at Jordan with a raised eyebrow.

"Yes," Jordan groaned, "the life talk."

"Yep, the life talk, about condoms and girls and holding out on being sexually active for as long as you can because of diseases and drama and jealousy? And that love and commitment should not be confused with lust and shacking up.

"If you find the right girl when you are in high school, you can wait for the sex. It's not going anywhere. Your penis won't fall off. Both of you can wait, get an education and a way to earn and then you can make a serious commitment."

"Yes." Jordan sighed. He would never forget the cringe-worthy conversation.

"It's good that you remember." Joseph squinted at him. "I depend on you to remember these things because I want you to be different you are never to repeat my mistakes. If my father had just one conversation with me about sex instead of me following my peers' stupidly, I would have a different life. I told you that I had my first sexual experience at fourteen?"

"Yes." Jordan avoided his father's eyes. "You told me."

"Parents are here to guide you in life." Joseph waited until he made eye contact again before speaking.

"I don't want to leave my duty as a guide especially

through this time of your life to anyone else. I won't do it to Preston either. I am going to find a way to be a proper father to him despite his mother."

Jordan bit back a groan. Two heavy conversations in one evening. He wondered how many other twelve-year-olds were subjected to adult introspection.

"Don't complain about it," Joseph laughed. "I wish my father was not as awkward about these things. As I said, it would have saved me a world of hurt. Some children grow up never really knowing their parents. You know parents try to hide their imperfections and mistakes from their children. They sometimes feel ashamed of what they had done and never speak out, but when their children repeat the same mistakes, they wished they had said something."

Jordan sighed. "Yes, sir."

"I will hide nothing from you guys." Joseph looked at Jordan fondly. "My boys will not make the same mistakes I did."

"First of all, that box," he pointed to a box which read important papers. "Contains the papers for the house, it is paid for, so you will always have somewhere to live— always. Nobody can blackmail you into marrying anyone because you don't have a roof over your head. It also has your name on the land title. Don't forget to pay the property taxes when you get older, okay."

Jordan nodded.

"The box also contains a joint fixed account I started years ago with the intention of leaving Jennifer, a wealthy man. It has some money in there.

"I opened it in both your moms and my name, I will add you tomorrow. It should mature when you are sixteen. I figure by then it will have enough money to pay for the college education of all three of you. I know Preston, Walter, and Saint are covered by their mother. I want you three to have the same opportunities that they will have."

Jordan grinned. "College? Really? Suppose I want to just go and work as a..."

"You are going to college," Joseph interrupted him. "I am going to send you to college. Nobody will be holding it over your head that they sent you to college; therefore, you have to marry their daughter."

Joseph growled, "Which means you cannot waste time in high school, Jordan."

"Yes, sir." Jordan nodded humbly. He finally saw where his father was going with this. He was putting right all that had gone wrong in his life. All that had brought him here to this point.

"And finally, girls." Joseph ran his hand over his face. "If you find one that you love and you want to spend the rest of your life with, you must marry her. Make it official. Having children with someone is not a legally binding commitment. If I had married your mother as soon as I could, I wouldn't have been free to marry Jennifer and... "

Jordan nodded slowly.

"I cannot wish away Preston, Walter, and Saint." Joseph sighed and leaned back in his chair. "I love them. They are my sons, but I could not continue living the way I was living, you know what I mean?"

"I think so," Jordan whispered.

"In this life there comes a time when you have to start choosing differently for your own well being."

"Yes Dad," Jordan said. He no longer wished that the conversation would end. He was getting a glimpse into his father's psyche the reason why he did things.

"You have to live your life," Joseph said, "I think it's finally time for me to be living my best life and I want to see my sons live theirs as well."

Chapter Eight

Miss Pam saved his Christmas holiday, Preston concluded, as he stared at her while she busied herself in the kitchen excitedly.

Without her, he and his brothers would not even be at home. They would have been stuck in the warehouse watching the frantic activity that would signal that the busiest time of the year was around the corner.

Christmas and impending hurricanes were the busiest times for supermarkets, and the business took precedence over celebrating the holiday as a family.

Even his parents called a truce. His father who had left the business in November was coerced back two weeks later for the holiday season. His mom had not found a replacement manager, and she was quite literally run off her feet. He hardly saw her these days, and he was thinking that wasn't a bad thing.

His mother made the house feel heavy and depressed

whenever she was around, and with her being so busy she forgot that she was in mourning. Her absence and preoccupation had a positive effect on everyone. Walter had started talking again, and Saint had finally stopped wetting the bed.

Preston didn't feel angry all the time, especially because his dad started dropping in more when his mother wasn't there, and they had real conversations.

Of course, he couldn't tell his mother about their quality time. They were sworn to secrecy, or they wouldn't see him again.

Preston sighed when he thought about it. She would eventually find out when she was less busy, then this period of normalcy would be over.

They were all gathered in the kitchen watching as Miss Pam baked her traditional Christmas puddings.

"Sheryl will be here tomorrow." Miss Pam looked at the three of them sternly. "You will treat her like a long lost and highly regarded sister."

They nodded dutifully. They would agree to anything— Miss Pam was doling out tiny morsels of fruit that was soaked in rum and allowing them to lick the cake mixture from the bowls. Preston was thinking that this was better than actually eating the cake. He didn't particularly like fruitcake but this ritual of baking and having them participate had him hooked.

She was finally finished and cleaning up when his father dropped in.

"Boys, Miss Pam." his father greeted them exuberantly.

He looked so happy it was clear for even the blind to see. He had never looked this happy when he was living with them.

He picked up Saint who was practically throwing himself at his dad like a puppy.

"Hi, Dad." Preston grinned. The sight of his dad was an added bonus to his already happy day.

"I am going home to change," his father looked over at him, "we are going to pick sorrel in the hills at my uncle's farm. I want you to come."

"Me?" Preston jumped up from the stool. He had no idea that his father had an uncle in the hills. He realized that he didn't know anything much about his father's family.

"Can I come too Daddy, please?" Walter started to plea, and Saint joined in.

"Not today, guys. Sorry." His father stooped down to be eye level with Saint. "Maybe next week when Mickey kills his annual Christmas goat. Only my older sons are coming with me today."

Preston's heart almost stopped beating. Did that mean that Jordan would be there too?

"Get dressed." His father raised an eyebrow at him. "Quickly."

He didn't have to say it twice. Preston ran out of the kitchen and then stopped, he was so excited he had forgotten which direction his room was in. There was a change in the air. He was going to spend more time with his dad and maybe have some more freedom away from his mother.

The thought was enough to make him dizzy.

****

They were squirming with excitement when his father stopped at the forbidden house.

The house of evil, according to his mother.

It was their first visit. It was access to his other life. There were so many things to take in at once. Preston looked around. It was much smaller than their house. One side of the fence was covered with bright bougainvilleas and the other with red poinsettias. The rest of the place was paved. There was a short walk to the main front door and a long narrow veranda and then the entrance to another side of the house where a sign read: *The Best Hair Salon.*

His father led them to the front door and opened it.

Preston took a deep gulp of air before he tentatively walked in with his dad. Walter and Saint clung to each arm. They were as nervous as he was.

Their mom had told them stories. He half expected bats to fly out through the door and lightning and thunder to greet them as they entered.

Instead, the hall was simply decorated, two boys were sitting on the floor, one was reading a book with his hand at his jaw, the other was playing with his toy trucks. They both greeted his father exuberantly and then went back to what they were doing.

The one closest to Walter in age looked at them curiously. He had very curly hair that was almost in his eyes. It looked like a mop.

The youngest boy was about the same age as Saint. He was impossibly cute. He looked doll-like.

Preston dragged his eyes from the boys and to his father who stood in the middle of the space like an impressive monument.

"Jordan get out here!"

"Coming Dad!" Jordan said from what Preston assumed was the bedroom area.

"Oh, you are here!" Hannah came through the other side of the hallway.

He knew it was Hannah. Nobody had to tell him. She was even more beautiful close up than he remembered and she smelled nice. She looked at him and his brothers and greeted them one by one, shaking their hands.

And then Jordan finally came out of the beaded archway and froze. His eyes were swinging from one to the other of them as if he could not believe his eyes.

His father inhaled audibly. "So, here you all are. I think it is time to introduce my boys to each other officially."

And that is how Preston and Jordan Wiley finally acknowledged their connection.

"Blood is thicker than water," Joseph Wiley said when they nodded at each other as if they were polite strangers, "never forget that."

****

Preston was on a high. The younger boys were dropped off at Hannah's sister, Monique. She was a lovely lady who reminded him of Hannah. She obviously loved children and animals. She was about to feed her peacocks. The place was like a wildlife reserve. He half envied his younger brothers for staying, but he felt privileged to be with the big boys.

His father and Jordan were hilarious together. They had the kind of rapport that he wished he had with his dad.

But he had no time to dwell on that though because his father drove them into a part of Portland that he had no idea existed—deep rural Portland with lush green trees and prehistoric-looking plants. He looked around in awe. He had watched Jurassic Park the night before, and the place looked eerily like it.

"You look scared." Jordan turned around from the front and grinned at him. "You have never been to the bush before, have you?"

"No." Preston shrugged and then grinned sheepishly. "I watched Jurassic Park last night. It does have that feel. Any minute now, I expect one of those T Rex to appear at the top of the trees."

His father laughed. "This place does have that feel, but the only dinosaurs up these parts is my great uncle, Mickey. He won't hurt you though."

Preston chuckled and settled back in his seat.

"You like dinosaurs, huh?" Jordan looked at him with interest. "So does Shawn, you two would get on very well together."

"Nah," Preston shook his head, "I am not sure I like them. Walter likes them more than me. He couldn't shut up about it today."

Jordan grinned. "I know what you mean. When Guy likes something, it is enough to drive me crazy. He read A Cow Called Boy and now he is suddenly fascinated with cows."

Preston nodded. "I know what you mean."

They started sharing their baby brother stories completely missing the pleased smile on their father's face.

Chapter Nine

By the New Year Preston had friends. He became a part of Jordan's group as soon as he stepped into the schoolyard in January. They had shared a few moments in the Christmas—a forbidden family get together with his father's people in the hills. He had lunch at Hannah's house, with his brothers when his mother was catching up on her sleep and on Boxing Day he ran wild with Jordan and Shawn, after his mother had come down with the flu, and couldn't monitor him as she usually would.

Miss Pam who was supposed to be supervising him was wholeheartedly for his new-found freedom, and she had no qualms keeping him mother-free for the duration. His one regret for the holiday was that he had not gotten the chance to get to know Miss Pam's daughter, Sheryl. She had pretty brown eyes. The whites of her eyes were pure and bright, and her irises were kind of like a dark mahogany. They were framed with chunky spiky thick lashes that seemed like they were clumped together. He had been feeling weird ever since he met her.

He would have examined the reason more if he had not been so caught up with his newly discovered family and the unprecedented freedom he had experienced over the holidays.

He felt...what was the word? Happy. He felt happy.

It showed in his walk. He had a swagger to his step as his strutted beside his brother into the classroom. He sat in his usual spot and Summer, the girl with the inquisitive attitude, gave him a knowing smile.

"You seem different."

"What do you mean?" he asked smugly.

"I don't know," Summer shrugged, "maybe less standoffish. What did you do this holiday?"

"None of your business," Preston said and then looked over at Jordan who gave him a half wave.

"Hey, can I sit over there?" he asked looking over Summer's head.

"Sure." Jordan nodded. "Otis will exchange places with you."

Otis sat at the desk immediately beside Jordan. Otis looked put out at the suggestion, but he shrugged and got up.

"You guys chat too much anyway. I will be happy to leave, especially if I am sitting beside Summer."

Preston got up with his bag and looked over at Summer. "Bye."

"Bye." Summer chuckled. "I see that the Wiley's have sorted out their family business."

Preston did not bother to answer. He walked over to what he called in his head, Jordan's Corner and sat in Otis' vacated chair. It felt right.

****

A few weeks later all was not as honky dory in Preston's world as it was during the Christmas holidays. His mother fully recovered from the flu and found a general manager for the business. Her second cousin Glenda's son, Fred Seaton.

Fred had been living in the Solomon Islands where he ran a supermarket. He had been itching to come back to Jamaica for a while, and this was his opportunity.

Fred moved into his father's suite at the house and into his new role at the business with seamless ease.

At first, Preston was not sure about Fred when he just met him. He was younger than he thought he would be. He was just twenty-five years old, and he looked it. He was tall slim and gangly and looked a lot like Marlon Wayans from the Wayans Brothers Show.

Maybe that was why Preston couldn't take him seriously at first, and he had wondered if his mother had gotten too desperate to find a general manager.

But then he warmed up to Fred.

Fred loved to play card games with them especially Uno. He encouraged Preston to talk about his other brothers, listening with interest and asking questions. He had a calming effect on his mother.

Fred was a welcomed addition to the house.

Miss Pam confirmed it one Sunday morning in February while he was eating breakfast with his brothers.

"I hope Fred doesn't find a nice woman and get married and move away from here." She winked at Preston. "I like him in this house. He adds balance to the somberness."

"But why would he move even if he finds someone?" Preston asked, "There is lots of space here."

Pam snorted. "Nobody would want to live here voluntarily. Your mother is a..."

She looked at the younger boys and corrected herself. "Your mother would not allow it."

She started wiping down the counters. "You haven't told her anything about seeing your other brothers have you?" She eyed the three of them with suspicion.

"No." Walter was the one who answered. "Daddy said if we did we wouldn't see him again."

"Good." Miss Pam pursed her lips, "a messed up situation if I ever saw one. I am almost reluctant to move Sheryl into this place. Even though your mother grudgingly agreed to it."

"Sheryl is going to move here?" Preston straightened up in his chair.

"Yes." Miss Pam sighed, "my mother is migrating—my brothers and sisters in the States arranged it, which means Sheryl will have to come here. I can't leave a twelve-year-old girl to live by herself in Kingston."

"She didn't like her Christmas holiday." Miss Pam made a face. "She is a town girl who hates the country, but she'll just have to get used to it."

Preston smiled. "We will make sure that she has a good time here and be her friend."

Miss Pam frowned. "That girl was born for greatness. Books will be her friend. Don't worry about good times. My girl is going to be a lawyer or a doctor or prime minister. Something big. I discourage her from having friends. I do not want her to be anything but the best."

Fred walked into the kitchen dressed in jeans and a white t-shirt. "You boys ready for school?"

"It's not a school day, Cousin Fred," Walter smirked at him.

"There are different types of school." Fred gave him a mock frown, "this school is sailing school. I am going to the marina. My friend Woody has a boat, that's one of the only things I can fault you Portlanders for, you are surrounded by sea, everybody should have a boat and yet some of you can't even swim. I can't leave my Wiley cousins with that incompetence."

"Yes!" Preston and Walter squealed together. "Sailing!"

Fred chuckled. "Your mother said yes, at least I think that is what she said through the room door."

"Jenny still sick, Pam?" Fred raised an eyebrow at Miss Pam.

Miss Pam shook her head and looked at them meaningfully.

That meant that they were about to have an adult conversation and they didn't want them to overhear.

Preston suppressed a sigh as if he didn't know. He heard his mother last night sobbing through her room door. Loud gasping sobs that had disturbed him enough that he had been unable to sleep.

She was not handling his dad's leaving well at all.

"I am not sick, Fred." His mother strolled into the kitchen. She looked very frail and thin since her bout with the flu. "I am just heartbroken."

She looked over at them at the nook and smiled. "My babies, good morning."

Saint got up and hugged her.

Preston and Walter murmured. "Good morning."

"Surely you greet your father with more enthusiasm than that." Jennifer sniped and walked over to the coffee pot. "He left us for another family. He is the enemy, not me."

Fred cleared his throat. "Jenny come on, it is a beautiful, sunny day..."

"What sun, I don't see any sun!" Jennifer snapped. "Did

you know that the other woman is pregnant? She is going to have an evil spawn."

"What is an evil spawn?" Saint asked brightly.

"An evil spawn is any child that your father has with that other woman, Hannah." Jennifer snapped.

"Is that a bad thing?" Saint was looking up at his mother intently.

"Yes!" Jennifer snarled. "It's the worse thing. Every time that woman procreates I die a little inside. All of them, all of her offspring are slowly killing your mommy."

"But I like Jordan and Guy and Case," Saint said innocently, "I didn't know they were killers."

The kitchen was still after that. Preston stiffened he knew what was coming. His mother turned a dark, unhealthy shade of red.

Miss Pam was rapidly doing a cross sign, and Fred was rubbing his temples.

"How do you know their names?" Jennifer sputtered.

"Because... er... they... er..." Saint clammed up. He realized what he had done. They had all been sworn to secrecy.

Preston knew that this would happen some time or the other. Saint was too little to keep secrets. He had expected this showdown a long time before now. It was a miracle that Saint had held off for three whole months since Christmas especially since he had such a good time over the holiday with their dad. His excitement had been infectious.

His mother looked at him and Walter knowingly. "The baby always spills the beans. I guess your father disobeyed me and introduced you to his other family."

Walter visibly swallowed.

Preston flinched when his mother looked at him. There was wildness in her eyes.

"Mom..." he began slowly, he wasn't sure what to say after

that.

"Did you meet her?" Jennifer asked calmly.

It wasn't the explosion that he feared. Preston contemplated not answering.

"Preston, Andre Wiley!" Jennifer leaned on the counter and folded her arms, her coffee forgotten.

"Jenny, this is not important," Fred began. "They are little boys why are you dragging them into this?"

Jennifer ignored Fred.

"Preston Andre Wiley! Will you lie to your mother now? Will you choose your father, the betrayer, over me?"

Her lips were trembling.

Preston felt his head swelling, his heart felt like a sledgehammer ringing against hard stone.

He swung his gaze to Miss Pam who was holding herself as still and as unobtrusively as possible. She would be no help. She had a job to keep.

"Who are you going to choose, Preston?" Jennifer's voice was no longer steady. "Are you going to tell me the truth?"

"I...I... don't know what to say." Preston stammered.

"Did you meet that man stealer, Hannah Kennedy?"

"No." Preston shook his head.

"Did you meet her children?" Jennifer had her hands clasped in fists at her side.

"I am in the same class with Jordan." Preston sidestepped the question. "I know him."

"Ah, Jordan." Jennifer nodded. " Are you two friends now? You say his name with such familiarity."

"Yes!" Preston lost his senses. This grilling was unfair. It was unjust. It was ridiculous. Why should he be caught in the crossfire that was his parents' lives?

"Yes, we are friends. I like him. He is my brother, and he is not evil, nor is he a killer. You shouldn't say those things to Saint. He is just a little boy!"

Jennifer widened her eyes. "Go to your room!"

Preston got up from around the table. "You are a terrible mother for saying the things you say and acting the way you act. I prefer Hannah to you. At least she is nice and kind, and she doesn't call Dad names!

"They have love in their house. In here is just a war zone where you bawl and howl and scream all day as if you are a mad woman!"

He didn't know where the gasps came from. Miss Pam was holding her mouth, and his mother had gone an unhealthy shade of deep purple. Not just her ears, her forehead, her neck.

Nor did he know what came over him. That was the worst insult ever to give his mother. This would cut deep.

Her eyes looked as if a light had gone out of it.

They were dead, bleak. He was in trouble. He almost expected her to explode right now. Instead, she turned her back to him and reached for her coffee cup.

"No sailing for them today, Fred." Her voice was almost even. "As a terrible mother, I have a reputation to maintain."

Chapter Ten

"Dad, she is following us again." Jordan turned to his father. They had gone to Port Antonio to a farm store for a routine shopping trip. His father had started a farming venture with his uncle Mickey, and they had gone to buy seeds and a present for Preston whose birthday was tomorrow. They had spent a pleasurable half hour in the electronics store after school, and they had settled on buying Preston a **Pokemon Gameboy.**

He had first realized that the black BMW that Jennifer Wiley drove was slowly trailing them over town. It was quite a feat. Port Antonio town was narrow and relatively small. The seawall was to one side, and the rest of the town was like a hodgepodge of buildings that were so close together and near the narrow road that parking in the middle of town was at times difficult.

But there she was. She drove around the circular street until they came out of the store and she parked beside them at the electronics store. And now she was quite obviously following them when they pulled out of town. His father's face was grim.

He clenched his fist on the steering wheel.

"She has been doing this for a while."

Jordan frowned. "Maybe you should tell the police."

Joseph looked over at him. "I already did. I had to file a restraining order against her a couple of weeks ago."

"But why is she still following?" Jordan looked back at the vehicle. He could see the outline of Jennifer Wiley's features but not her expression. What was going on here?

"She is acting slightly erratic." Joseph sighed, "It seems as if she has gone a little bit over the edge."

"Is she dangerous?" Jordan whispered, still craning his head to look back at the vehicle. His father picked up speed as they passed the ruins of the Folly Great House and the beautiful edifice of the Trident Hotel, which looked as if it were being hugged, by the sea.

He usually admired the place from a distance. For him, it was the best part of leaving Port Antonio while heading into the more rural area of Drapers.

His father's response was to pick up speed, and the BMW doggedly followed. It felt like something out of a movie as his father tried to outrun his wife.

They were fairly evenly matched: his father's 1996 Jeep Cherokee and Jennifer's BMW. It became somewhat of a race to the death as they screeched along the main road. The sea whizzed by in a blur, and then the sea gave way to greenery as they headed into the stretch to Drapers.

Jordan vacillated between excitement and horror. His father was clenching his jaw and looked like this was a death match.

They arrived at Drapers Square, which was just a collection

of small shops and a small plaza, his father pulled over in front of Miss Jean's Patty and Cocoa bread shop. Jennifer pulled over too with tires screeching.

"Stay in the car." His father warned as he got out.

Jordan obeyed, but he had a good view of the ensuing conflict. Miss Jennifer got out of the car too; she didn't look as ruffled as her driving had indicated. She didn't even slam her car door.

"Leave me alone." His father growled. "Please Jennifer."

"You leave Hannah Kennedy alone," Jennifer said loud enough for Jordan and the smattering of curious people in the vicinity to hear. "Leave her, and I will forgive you for all of this. Tomorrow is Preston's birthday; our son is turning thirteen, that's a big deal in a boy's life. You can come home and be with your rightful, legitimate family. And all will be happy again."

His father folded his arms and regarded her before answering. "We were never happy. You got the restraining order, Jennifer?"

It was as if all the bands of civil behavior that had been holding her together snapped. Jennifer pointed at his father. "You cannot restrain me. I am your wife!"

"Jennifer," his father said calmly, "please stop following me around."

"You are going to pay for humiliating me this way," Jennifer growled. "I am not letting you go so easily. Till death do us part, Joseph Wiley."

She got into the car and reversed from the square.

His father walked slowly back to the car and got in.

In typical Portland fashion, the rain started in earnest, and they sat in silence while Jennifer's threat sunk in.

Jordan looked at the rivulets of water as it coated the windshield. He felt a premonition of doom so strong it frightened him.

"We should move from here." He said it feverishly, his eyes wide and frightened.

"No." Joseph shook his head. "I can handle Jennifer. She is not as scary as she acts. Don't worry son. We are not in any danger."

Jordan realized that his father was not taking his fears seriously and the feeling of dread continued for the rest of the evening.

Jordan didn't eat his dinner. He pushed it around his plate eventually giving most of it to Guy who had not a care in the world.

He listened as his mother discussed the new baby.

"It's a girl." She was excited. "Finally a girl. I am going to name her something Biblical. I like the name Athaliah."

"Or Jezebel," Case said innocently.

His parents and Guy laughed. Jordan could not find any humor in the situation even though it was funny.

"Jezebel was not a very nice lady," Hannah said to Case. "I thought since you go to church every week you'd know this."

Joseph grinned. "Maybe that is what Tate is preaching to them. "

"Maybe I should ask Adalynn about this." Hannah mused.

"If something were to happen to you who would take care of us?" Jordan asked his parents seriously.

Hannah looked at him with a frown.

Joseph shook his head in rebuke. "Jordan, you still feel uncomfortable about today?

"It is a good question." Jordan felt a knot in his stomach, "I don't feel right inside. I think something bad is going to happen."

"Oh baby," His mother came around to his side of the table

and hugged him. "Nothing is going to happen to us. Why on earth would you feel this way? It was just one encounter with a woman who is slightly unhinged. Nothing more."

Tears pricked Jordan's eyes. "I don't know why I just feel weird."

"Well, shake yourself out of it." Hannah gripped his chin and smiled in his eyes. "Nothing is going to happen. Our family is finally together, and in four months you will have a baby sister to spoil. Which reminds me, you and your father will have to clean out the storeroom. It will make a perfect girls room."

"And if anything happens," his father said solemnly, acknowledging the impact his encounter with Jennifer may have had on him, "you have your aunt, Monique. Stop fretting about the future. You are a child. It's not your place to fret about these things."

"Besides that, we are young." Hannah smiled at him. "I am looking forward to seeing you grow up and to get married and make me a grandmother."

****

Jennifer Wiley struck the next day, midday April 26, Preston's birthday. She followed her husband to his home in Drapers and shot him at the gate. He was still in his vehicle. Just about to come out. She got him in the chest.

She then walked calmly into Hannah's hairdressing parlor and shot her in the belly and the head. Hannah was attending to a customer, her sister Monique and she too was hit.

And then Jennifer shot herself.

They were calling it the Drapers Massacre. The whole countryside was in shock. Jordan, Preston, and Shawn were walking to the bus stop when Preston excitedly told them about his birthday cake that Miss Pam had baked which was in the shape of a house, with its own roof and everything.

They hardly paid attention to the chatter around them as the busmen, and the taxi drivers huddled around and discussed the horrendous crime in Drapers.

It was Shawn who stopped when she heard the name, Jennifer Wiley. And then the taxi man continued, "first she shot the husband, then she shot the husband's girlfriend and then the girlfriend's sister and then she shot herself. All of them dead. Though I think the husband was rushed to the hospital. Not sure if he is alive".

Jordan was the first one to notice Shawn's absentmindedness and the look of sick horror on her face.

"Shawn, what's wrong?" Jordan swung around. "Come on. We have to go home and get Preston's gift."

Shawn was just standing there and was visibly trembling.

It was Preston who realized that there was a sort of stillness descending on the park. Most of the conversations were dying off, and everybody was looking at them.

"What's wrong?" His voice was weak when he finally spoke, and then he realized that Jordan was standing as still as a statue and staring at Shawn who had not yet moved.

"My mom?" Jordan asked weakly still staring at Shawn.

Shawn nodded and then slowly came forward, "and your mom, she pointed to Preston. "And Monique and your dad."

"No," Jordan shook his head, "stop this."

"Your dad is in hospital, but he may not make it."

"What is she talking about?" Preston felt a band tighten around his chest and his head felt loads bigger than his body.

"Your mom killed them all and then killed herself," Shawn whispered. "I think she killed Aunt Monique too."

Their regular bus driver, Charlie came beside them and touched Preston on his shoulders. "Miss Pam said I should take you home."

"Jordan, come with me too, I'll take you to Shawn's house yours is...come on, let's get out of here."

Charlie had to push Preston into the bus forcibly. He could not move. His feet were not obeying him. His head was overcrowded with so much bad news he couldn't process it.

****

His thirteenth birthday evening was hell for Preston. What was supposed to be a celebration was mourning.

He was sitting in the half dark living room while Fred spoke to the doctor in the foyer.

Once again it hit him. He was an orphan. He had no parents. His mother had killed his father and two other people. This was too much for anyone to deal with much less a boy who had just turned thirteen.

He had hoped for the fifteen minutes between Port Antonio and Drapers that it wasn't true. Shawn and Jordan had wailed all the way nonstop, and he had sat there in denial. *His mother would never do what they said. She didn't even own a gun. It was his birthday. His mother had them to live for.*

The news was one of those crazy rumors that had no basis in reality.

He held on to his delusions until the very last minute, until Charles left him at the gate and he saw Miss Pam standing in the driveway her face tear-streaked and puffy. Her eyes were red.

"Be strong, son," Charlie had said as he reversed out of the driveway.

That's when he started to cry, enveloped in Miss Pam's arms. Throughout the evening when his brothers had come home, fresh bursts of grief had overtaken him especially after Walter walked in and headed for the living room with his school bag still on his back.

He hadn't taken it off since. He refused to let anyone touch him. He sat in the corner of the settee trembling and staring into space. He had gone mute again.

Seeing his brother so pitiful moved Preston to tears and that had set Saint off.

"When is Mommy coming home?" he asked sniffling.

Walter had curled up in the settee and turned his back to them. And Preston had to comfort his little brother.

"Mommy is never coming home again." He had told a sniffling Saint.

Preston was happy that Saint had eventually cried himself to sleep, curled up in the settee beside him.

Fred was busy with a million and one phone calls and now the doctor. They stood whispering in the foyer.

Miss Pam had to handle visitors. It seemed as if the gate bell rang every ten seconds.

The doctor was their regular doctor, Dr. Hill. She had dealt with Walter before when he went silent.

Walter took one look at her as she leaned over him and started to sob. Big heartbroken sobs that almost triggered Preston's tears again.

He overheard the doctor talking about a regular routine and keeping visitors and conversations about the deaths to a minimum, especially with insensitive people. And he heard Miss Pam agreeing.

Then Fred came into the living room and scooped Saint up to put him to bed and Walter was given a sedative and taken to his room because once he had started crying, he couldn't stop.

And then it was just him in the living room. He refused

help. He was a big boy. He was a teenager. What an initiation into the turbulent years this was.

He spared a thought for Jordan, Guy, and Case. He wondered what kind of chaos was going on at their house. He wondered if they had removed the bodies yet. He wondered if Jordan would ever talk to him again. He wondered if he had caused this madness. He could have.

He had told his mother that she was terrible and that Hannah was better.

Dear God, I caused her to go over the edge. All of this is my fault.

He rested back on the sofa as Fred came into the room and sat across from him.

"Do not worry about anything, Preston. Glenda is taking the first flight she can out of Trinidad where she was on business. Other family members and friends are offering their support. In the long haul, you boys have me. I am going nowhere. I'll always be here for you. Hopefully, my life will be spared to see you past the worst."

Preston nodded.

Fred sighed and sat back in his chair. "I am still in disbelief, but I'll try my best to be present for you, okay."

Preston closed his eyes. "Thanks, Fred."

"This is a rough birthday," Fred whispered. "You want anything to eat?"

"No thanks." Preston squeezed out the answer amid a suddenly dry throat.

They sat together in silence for a long while.

There were other visitors, the police and Fred left to attend to them and then there was another visitor, a friend of Miss Pam's.

Preston could hear them through the kitchen almost clearly.

"Why would Miss Jennifer do such a thing?" Miss Pam

sobbed. "Why couldn't she just move on with her life? Joseph Wiley was just a man. Why couldn't she just leave him alone? Now she has taken four lives along with hers."

"Which four, I thought it was three?" Preston heard the friend ask.

"Miss Hannah and her unborn baby, Mr. Joseph, and Miss Monique," Miss Pam said hoarsely, "not to mention that she left behind six boys without parents, Miss Monique's three children are motherless. Who is going to take care of Jordan, Guy and Case? Especially Case, the kid is just six."

The friend sighed. "Monique was the one who grew Hannah and Sharla when their mother disappeared, and their father died."

"So they have nobody." Miss Pam groaned, "Monique is dead, her husband is dead."

"I guess his family will step in for the children." the friend added. "Their big brother is Toddy Pryce, the senator. He had a soft spot for Monique. He allowed her to live on the farm even though the other siblings wanted to kick her off."

"But who will be there for those little boys, the ones that Jennifer robbed of their mother and father?" Miss Pam grunted. "Who? If she wasn't already dead, I would knock some sense into that woman."

"Pam!" Fred interrupted sternly, "take this conversation away from here! Preston is in the living room he can hear you."

"His mother should have thought of that before she killed so many people." The friend said snidely. "You can't protect him from the talk, Fred. He will be hearing this and worse in the days and years to come. People just can't help feeling some sort of way about this."

Chapter Eleven

They buried three people the same Sunday: Joseph Wiley, Hannah Kennedy and Monique Kennedy Pryce in the same family plot. Jennifer Wiley had been buried the Wednesday before in a very private ceremony.

Jordan stood with his hands around Guy throughout the burial service. He had to be strong for him. Shawn and her mother stood beside them. His aunt Sharla and her husband Tanner flanked them.

The rain held up for the long service, nearly six hours of speeches and songs. He was exhausted.

It was ironically a bright, beautiful day. The kind of day that he would be spending with his dad in the hills or swimming at the Blue Hole.

And now there was no dad. He was the last to be buried.

The minister intoned. "Ashes to ashes, dust to dust."

The choruses were sung. The mourners mourned. And then it was over.

Guy cried. Case was standing still, wide-eyed and curious under a cousin's arms. He didn't understand what was happening. He thought that their parents were going to return.

Jordan had been crying on and off for the three weeks before the funeral and was all cried out for now on the actual day of saying goodbye.

The counselor at school told him that he would probably grieve for the rest of his life but at a different intensity.

He believed her.

The counselor also said he shouldn't carry bitterness and blame for Jennifer Riddley. But he did. He felt such a deep sense of hatred and anger that he felt like hitting something or someone. That woman had robbed him of his parents and his sister and his precious aunt.

He looked over at Preston, Walter, and Saint, all of them standing in their funeral finery while their mutual father was lowered into the ground. He had to force himself not to blame them for this.

It wasn't their fault.

He couldn't fault them, but he desperately wanted to.

When it was over, he walked beside Shawn to the waiting cars.

Shawn was in an identical tux to his. She looped her hand through his. "Aren't you going to say anything to Preston and the other boys?"

Jordan looked at her sharply. "No. Shouldn't they be the ones saying something to me and Guy and Case?"

"Dude, it must be tough for them to be at the funeral of the people their mother killed, plus their own father. I reckon they are feeling pretty awful too, probably more than you."

Shawn stopped walking and forced him to stop with her.

"So why did they come?" Jordan growled. "Why didn't

they stay home, holed up in their ivory tower while the rest of us get on with it."

"Because they are family." Shawn looked at him with compassion. "Joseph Wiley was their father too. I don't want you bitter, Jordan. Too many bitter feelings and craziness have happened in your family already. The six of you are all that's left of Joseph Wiley. You guys are going to have to get along and be a different family. You will have to do the opposite of what Miss Jennifer wanted with her hate."

Jordan narrowed his eyes and looked at Shawn. It was a very wise thing to say. It cut through his grief and made him think. *When did Shawn get so wise?* He was usually the voice of reason in their friendship.

He glanced across the fresh mound of graves. Preston was standing at the same place that he was standing earlier. His hands were in his pockets. He was hunched over and looking stiff and lonely as if he were the only person on the planet like all the stuffing had been battered out of him.

And Jordan suddenly realized that for him it must be harder. His mother had allowed hate to overwhelm her. His mother was the cause of all of this. He must feel a tremendous sense of loss.

"Ignoring him won't help," Shawn murmured. "You ignored him last week at school. The whole school ignored him. You know what he told me? He said he wished that his mother had killed him too."

Jordan gasped. "Really, he said that?"

Shawn nodded. "I think out of all of you; it hit him the hardest. You need to look after him, Jordan. Make a pact or something that you'll always look out for each other."

Jordan exhaled and then unhooked his hand from Shawn's. "He is the older one. He should be the one to do this."

"He is older; you are bolder." Shawn smiled. "Go on."

"We wouldn't be in this predicament if their mother hadn't killed mine," Jordan muttered a streak of stubbornness holding him back. What Shawn was asking was that he committed himself to these brothers that he barely knew. Suppose one of them was like their crazy mother?

He rubbed his hand over his eyes and looked behind, Guy and Case were surrounded by concerned family. He allowed them to get all the fussing they could. It was going to be a tough road ahead for them.

He still didn't know what their future would hold.

His closest family was Aunt Sharla, and she lived in Canada. Shawn's mother Jackie had moved into their house after the shooting three weeks ago and had continued with the shop.

He didn't know if she would continue to live with them, he doubted that. He didn't know if Jackie was the best parental figure in the world. How would she manage three additional children?

He sighed.

"Go talk to him." Shawn pushed him. He almost stumbled.

He glared at her. "Okay already. Though I don't know what on earth I could say."

Jordan headed to Preston who was watching the gravediggers as they did their finishing work.

Jordan approached him from behind and touched him on the shoulders.

Preston spun around frightened. His eyes were blood red. His cheeks still had undried tear streaks.

"Hey," Jordan said awkwardly standing beside him and mimicking his pose.

Preston's face crumpled. "I am so sorry, Jordan. This is all my fault."

"How can it be your fault?" Jordan frowned. He didn't

expect the utter despair he heard in Preston's voice or the defeat in his stance.

"I told my mom that she was terrible and that your mom was nicer." Preston hiccupped. "I should have known she couldn't handle hearing something like that. She killed them on my birthday. It was a message to me."

Jordan put his hand around Preston's shoulders. "It's not your fault. It can't be."

Preston started sobbing in earnest, which made Jordan tear up.

"I am sorry too."

"For what?" Preston sniffed and looked at him.

"For ignoring you these past couple of weeks."

"I understand." Preston swallowed.

"I won't ever do it again," Jordan said as Preston started to sob in earnest. "I'll always look out for you. You, Walter, Saint, Guy, Case are now my responsibility."

"And mine." Preston sniffed. "I am the firstborn."

Jordan nodded. "You are, but just by a little."

Preston sobbed noisily.

Jordan tightened his arms around him. "You will stop blaming yourself for what happened, and you will talk to me whenever you feel bad, okay?"

Preston blew his nose noisily and then looked at Jordan. "Only if you do the same."

"Okay." Jordan inhaled. "It's a deal."

****

After the funeral, there was a meeting chaired by Tate in his home library. His place was considered neutral ground and the perfect place to hash out the situation of the nine orphan children that they had on their hands.

The attendees sat on opposite sides of the room facing each other. All of them were in a somber mood.

Fred Seaton and his mother Glenda Blair sat on one side with their lawyer Norman Bradford. Sharla Phipps and her husband Tanner Phipps sat on the same side as Jonathan Toddy Pryce and his wife, Brandy Pryce.

Tate Griffith cleared his throat. "Well, it has been a challenging day and a very horrifying three weeks. We have been keeping Monique's girls, Giselle, Tiana, and Elsa and let me just say I have no idea how she made it look so effortless to care for triplets."

Toddy Pryce cleared his throat. "Brandy and I are willing to take them off your hands. In fact, we came here today prepared to take them. We have the means and the space to accommodate three girls."

"And the love," Brandy piped in. "I have a little girl myself, what is three more?"

Tate was assailed with doubt about this couple. Toddy Pryce was a big blustery fellow in his early fifties with political ambitions. Brandy was his third trophy wife who looked as if she didn't have one deep thought in her head. She looked like she had recently left her childhood behind, but he wouldn't judge.

Tate corrected himself hurriedly. *Looks can be deceiving. Not because Brandy looked like she spent a good chunk of the day in her mirror concentrating on herself meant that she did.*

Besides, Toddy Pryce was the only family member on the Pryce's side of the family who had come to the funeral and was even remotely interested in his baby sisters.

"Very well," Tate said out loud. "Adalynn will get them ready for you to take back with you to Kingston. We hope that you can keep in touch with us. Let us know how they are doing."

"For sure." Toddy nodded. "Definitely, pastor. I know that you were close to Monique. She often spoke of your wife as her best friend."

"Yes." Tate nodded. "Adalynn is in deep mourning. We considered keeping the girls but with two of our own..."

"No need to explain," Toddy aid politely, "we have this covered. I am a veteran at raising children. I have four, and they all did well in school and are upstanding citizens with a social conscience. My oldest, Lincoln, is currently entering the political fray because he wants to help people. They have grown up to be a credit to their mothers and me."

Tate nodded. "That is good to hear."

He inhaled and looked from Glenda and Fred to Sharla and Tanner. "That leaves the boys."

"Well," Norman Bradford cleared his throat. "I am here on behalf of the Riddley Estate. According to Gus Riddley's will, if Joseph Wiley divorced his wife, or died before his wife Jennifer Riddley Wiley, then all the shares in the business would go to her.

"However if Jennifer Wiley died before her husband the shares of the business and all other assets should be shared up equally among the Wiley children."

"Which Wiley children?" Sharla asked sharply.

"The Will did not say." Norman shook his head, "which technically would mean all the Wiley children. And since Jennifer Wiley died before her husband according to the time of death then I guess that means that all the properties and businesses that originally belonged to Gustavos Riddley would now belong to all the boys, even Hannah Kennedy's sons."

"And as the closest family to Gus and Jennifer, we will not contest it," Glenda said quickly. "I think it is only equitable since my cousin Jennifer's actions have caused massive devastation in their lives."

"If only Jennifer Wiley could see that her precious possessions were now equally shared by Hannah Kennedy's sons, it would surely kill her again, and she would deserve it." Sharla growled. "That bitch took away my two sisters that evil witch..."

She started sobbing again, and everybody sat uncomfortably while she wept. She shrugged off her husband's hand when he made to comfort her.

"I would kill her if she hadn't killed herself," Sharla growled. "I would easily just..."

"Come now Sharla," Tate said gently. "I know this is hard, I know this will take some time to get over but the boys are our priorities now, not thoughts of revenge."

"What can I do?" Sharla asked, her voice trembling, "I just moved to Canada, I just had a child of my own. I don't have a job yet. Tanner just switched jobs. We live in a bachelor apartment. Property in Toronto is like stupidly high priced. We don't have the money to buy a house right now. We cannot take on three boys."

"If I may?" Glenda said calmly. "I have a suggestion that may be a little unorthodox."

Sharla nodded. "I am listening."

"They could all live at the house. Pamela Stone is an efficient helper. We could increase her salary make it worthwhile for her to stay and keep an eye out for them. She could provide that motherly touch."

"And I'll be there," Fred said. "I already run the supermarket. I could sign an official guardian document or something."

Norman cleared his throat. "That can be arranged. In five years Preston and Jordan will be eighteen they can make decisions about their company then. You can be the stand-in until that time. You can make all decisions on behalf of the boys."

"Wait a minute!" Sharla growled, "I am not going to let my nephews move into that witches houses and be taken care of by her maid and cousin."

"The alternative is foster care," Glenda said, "I travel too much to take on children. I won't be a viable caregiver."

"Foster care?" Sharla whispered. "I wouldn't want Hannah's children to go into foster care. What about Joseph's family in the hills?"

"They would take the boys," Tate said, "but I would not recommend it. The conditions up there are not that great. Besides, Joseph's Uncle Mickey does not believe in education. He thinks it is a fancy way to brainwash young children and he thinks that churches and government institutions are a part of a wider conspiracy to turn people into zombies."

Sharla widened her eyes in horror. "Okay then."

"It is just five years until Preston and Jordan reach the age of majority," Glenda said. "The boys need to stick together. I would hate to see them being shuffled from foster home to foster home."

Sharla slumped her shoulders. "Okay."

"And Fred will be responsible for paying for their schooling and well being with money from the business. They should want for nothing." Glenda sighed, "Except parents of course, which is unfortunately why we are here."

"Indeed." Tate Griffith sighed, "and as for us, my wife and I are willing to offer support both spiritual and mental. My wife is a licensed psychologist who will be there for them when they need to talk, and I will always be around for anything they may need. The boys will be in good hands."

"So it's decided then?" Glenda said, relief in her voice. "I have a plane to catch later on this evening. I have been here for three weeks my company in Trinidad has been understanding under the circumstances, but it is time to move on."

Sharla nodded. "We have to leave too, tomorrow. I guess this solution is workable."

Chapter Twelve

This summer was a new era. It was unlike any summer before in his life. He was thirteen and on his own.

Jordan settled down in his hammock and tried not to think about how he got here. It was arranged that they would live in the Riddley's mansion with Miss Pam as their caretaker and Fred as their guardian.

He had refused.

He didn't want to leave his father's house. He didn't want to leave where he was, and nobody could convince him. They hadn't had the time anyway. They thought that everybody would just fall in with their plans, but they hadn't factored him in.

His aunt Sharla had gone back to Canada worried about him.

But he could take care of himself. He practically did most things by himself before his parents' death, except to cook. His mother had been determined that he would be independent. He hadn't grown up with maids like Preston and the other boys, he hadn't been pampered, and he didn't intend to start now.

Besides, Jackie checked in on him pretty often, and she paid him rent for the parlor.

Fred sent weekly groceries from the supermarket. He ate breakfast with Preston, lunch at school, and dinner at Pastor Tate's house.

Now, since the summer holidays, he just ate at Preston's. Miss Pam was a good cook, and she always left food for him or pressed him to eat. It was just easier to give in.

He slept in his own bed at home. That was non-negotiable.

Sometimes he missed his parents with an intensity that was terrifying. Not even Pastor Tate's prayers or Miss Adalynn's counseling could quell the yearning he felt for them.

But life went on.

It was the first full day of summer; Jordan sat on the bank of the Blue Hole with Shawn and Preston and Miss Pam's daughter Sheryl.

It was Sheryl's first day of the holiday. Preston had begged him and Shawn to include Sheryl in their little jaunts around the countryside. Preston wanted them to make things so interesting for her she would not miss Kingston.

They were on their best behavior for Sheryl today. He had not carried the younger brothers with them; it was just the four of them.

Jordan cracked an eyelid and looked at Sheryl. He wasn't so sure that she would survive Portland. She was prissy and complained about everything: the heat, the mosquitoes, leaves that fell from trees, the unpredictable weather. She was as jumpy as a yo-yo, and she would not go near the edge of the water because she feared alligators.

The Blue Hole in Portland was one of the worlds foremost

rafting sites that people came from far and near to enjoy, and Sheryl was afraid of alligators. He wasn't so sure she was a genius as Preston had said. Just because she was a class ahead of them and a year younger didn't mean squat if she thought alligators were in the Blue Lagoon.

Today she was in a little floral dress. She had a matching headband around her hair, which was plaited into long ropes down her back. She was as feminine and delicate as a wilting flower in the sunlight. She had medium brown skin and very unusual looking brown eyes with a black ring around them.

Preston had said they looked like mahogany and that she was model-pretty. Jordan stopped himself from snorting. She was just okay. Maybe if she were not afraid of imaginary alligators, she would look better.

Shawn wasn't afraid of anything. She was in the water floating. If she met an alligator, she would probably encourage the thing to try and eat her and then wrestle it into submission.

"Hey, Boojie Wiley," Shawn called from the water. "Want me to teach you how to swim?"

"No thanks." Preston who was at the water's edge answered. "I know how to swim."

"So come on in. Don't be standoffish like the town girl."

Preston looked over at Jordan, an exasperated expression on his face. He had begged Jordan to talk to Shawn about being on her best behavior.

Of course, Shawn was being Shawn, and there was nothing that he could do about it.

Jordan closed his eyes again. He was in a sweet spot under an almond tree. The breeze was just right. He wasn't feeling like going into the water just yet.

Sheryl came to sit near him. He heard her rustling as she arranged her towel on the rocks so that she didn't touch the rock. So girlish, he wasn't going to like her.

"I like Shawn." She announced to Jordan.

Jordan's eyes flew open. "You like Shawn?"

"I think she is a nice girl but very very rough around the edges. I think she'll make a nice friend."

Jordan chuckled. "How did you figure out that Shawn is a girl? You know Preston still thinks Shawn is a boy."

"Shawn is a girl?" Preston's shocked question echoed around them.

"Yep." Shawn hauled herself from the water and sat down beside Jordan.

"But your hair." Preston pointed to the curls plastered to her scalp. "You wear boys clothes. You wear khaki pants to school...you mean you don't have a...you know?" Preston had difficulty putting his thoughts together.

Shawn chuckled. "Yep, I don't have a penis. By the way, my days of wearing pants to school are over. The school found out that I am female and just like that I will have to wear a dress next year. It's truly unfair. Now the boys are going to be afraid to punch me in the boxing ring.

"Next thing you know I'll be talking all preppy like town girl here and wearing makeup and those things. Yuck."

Preston still looked gobsmacked.

Sheryl giggled. "It is obvious that Shawn is a girl, Preston. I could see it, and I just met her. If she weren't a girl, she would be a very pretty or feminine looking boy."

"No, it was not obvious." Preston shuddered. "You fight boys. You walk like a boy. You talk like one. Your voice is deeper than mine."

"So?" Shawn stuck her tongue out at him. "Girls have husky voices. I like mine. Jackie said I would do well on afternoon radio."

"Jordan said you were his other brother." Preston continued.

"He said you were his favorite brother!"

"And I am." Shawn laughed, "you jealous?"

"I was when I thought you were a boy." Preston shrugged, "now I just feel sad that Jordan has five brothers and yet his favorite brother is a girl who he isn't even related to."

Sheryl laughed. "That was funny."

Shawn got up and stretched. "You'll get over it. Jordy and I are practically twins. We just never made it from the same womb. Now I am going to swim out to where you see that log. If any of you think you can beat a mere girl you are welcomed to try."

Preston jumped up, a battle light in his eye. "Bring it on."

Shawn laughed. "Do you see how disinterested Jordan is to compete? That's because I beat him every time."

Jordan ignored them and closed his eyes again.

Shawn won. He heard her squeals of triumph above Preston's plea for a rematch.

Sheryl folded her hands in her lap. "Tell me what your high school is like."

"The same as high schools everywhere, just prettier." Jordan mused. He looked up into the cloudless sky. "You'll love it."

"I don't know." Sheryl mused, "I loved where I was. It was an all-girls school. The Queens School for girls."

"All girls?" Jordan sat up and looked at her.

"Yup, no stinky boys." Sheryl sighed, "and I was top of my class, and I sang in my school choir. You have a school choir?"

"Yep." Jordan nodded. "We do. "

"Have they won any awards?" Sheryl asked again, knitting her brows.

"Not that I know of," Jordan said apologetically. "I would love to go to an all-girls school."

"Ha," Sheryl snickered. "They would probably love to have you. You are cute and Preston too. When I saw him first, I literally said wow in my head."

"You did?" Jordan grinned. "I am going to tell him."

Sheryl smiled. "Please don't."

She turned her head away and watched Shawn and Preston for a while and then turned back to him. "I am sorry to hear about your situation. I can't imagine how sad it must be for you."

Jordan didn't answer. What could he say? The situation was beyond tragic.

"My dad died when I was eight," Sheryl murmured, "some moron shot him while he was on the job."

"He was a cop?" Jordan got interested in the conversation again. He was toying with the idea of being a cop or a soldier or a carpenter or maybe an engineer. He wasn't sure which one but being a cop was on his list.

"He was a good one too." Sheryl sighed. "I remember when he died I cried for days. I just couldn't deal with it."

Jordan cleared his throat. He wasn't in the mood to talk about death and crying and all of that anymore.

"Tell me about Kingston. What was it like living in the city?"

Sheryl's face lit up. That was her favorite topic, obviously. She paused in the telling when Preston and Shawn came to join them, and she took over the day with her accounts of Kingston and the places she had been to and the things she had done.

Preston was hanging on to her every word. It all made Jordan feel sleepy.

Chapter Thirteen

It was April 26, 1999, the first anniversary of their parents' death, and his birthday. Preston started the day with a heaviness that hugged him tight like a vice since he got up and saw the gray dawn sky.

One year went by so fast with so many changes; he was finding it hard to remember how it was before.

Everything had irrevocably changed. In some ways, he liked the changes, like the fact that he lived with Sheryl and four brothers instead of two, even though she was more interested in books than them. It meant that he had more people to play games with. He did not get the chance to feel lonely.

He also had more chores to do now. Miss Pam was determined that they grow up self-sufficient, and each of them, him, Walter and Guy had to take turns looking out for Case because he was the youngest.

Walter had started high school last year, and Guy would begin in the coming term. They all hoped that he would pass for Titchfield; it would make life easier if all four Wiley boys were going to the same place.

Four of them would be in high school.

He still found it amazing that Walter had managed to pass his external examinations after the trauma of last year's deaths. Not only had he passed but he had been the boy with the top science grades in their parish.

Preston still felt a fissure of pride when he thought about it. It had taken Walter three weeks to speak after last year's tragedy. Apparently, the trauma had not shut down his brain.

Preston reluctantly got ready for school that morning without any joy. The usual morning rain was pelting outside. It was April after all, Portland was known for its morning rain. It usually cleared up shortly after it started so he wasn't worried.

His days were pretty busy. Between school, home chores, after-school football club, which he only joined because of Jordan, and school choir rehearsal, which he joined because of Sheryl, he did not have the time to feel very sorry for himself.

He needed to drop one of his extracurricular activities though. He was becoming overwhelmed with all the things he had to do. Before he quit anything, he had to make sure that he wasn't feeling overwhelmed by negative thoughts because this was near the time of the deaths. He saw the school counselor every other Wednesday. She had warned him that he would face these feelings this morning.

Boy was she right.

"Cheer up, it's your birthday," Miss Pam said when he hauled himself to the kitchen and told them a dull good morning.

Sheryl was already there sitting around the table in her navy and white school uniform. She had her hair in her usual style: a high ponytail with a matching navy headpiece holding it aloft.

She was reading, her newly acquired glasses perched on her face. Her breakfast which looked like callaloo and green bananas was untouched.

Just a look at her would have him feeling peppier but not today.

Today his massive crush on Sheryl could not curb his sadness.

"Happy birthday," Sheryl looked up at him from her book and smiled.

"Thanks, but I don't think my birthday will ever be happy again," Preston mumbled. He sat down as Miss Pam served him his breakfast along with a glass of orange juice.

"At least drink your juice," Miss Pam warned him.

"Okay," Preston picked up the juice and sipped it. It was very tart. The oranges must have come from the sourest tree on the property. Nobody troubled that tree.

"You can put a spoon of sugar in it," Miss Pam said watching his expression.

He quickly did as she suggested.

Jordan walked into the kitchen just when he finished his juice and was looking balefully at his plate. He hated callaloo, but Miss Pam insisted on giving them vegetables.

Jordan had a brightly wrapped box tucked under his arm.

He pulled it out and brushed it off. "Morning everyone," Jordan said brightly. "It's a good thing Shawn let me borrow her bicycle or else I would have gotten wet. I have got to fix my tires."

Jordan came over to the house some mornings so that he could eat breakfast with them and get a ride to school with

Fred.

"Happy birthday big brother," Jordan said to him, putting down the box in front of the plate.

"This was your present from last year. Dad and I went driving all over town for it. I think Dad even wrote a letter or something. It's taped on the box. I found it in his room some months ago, thought it was best to give it to you on your birthday."

Tears welled up in Preston's eyes.

"Don't you dare cry," Jordan growled. "You are fourteen now."

"That was such a nice gesture, Jordan." Sheryl had tears running down her face.

Miss Pam was sniffling.

Jordan backed out of the kitchen. He wasn't comfortable with the emotions and was feeling choked up well. "I have to go check on Case."

Preston wiped his streaming eyes and sat staring at the box.

"It won't eat you," Fred said sitting down in front of him with a fresh cup of coffee in his hand.

Preston looked up at Fred, and he looked blurry. He wiped his eyes and then inhaled. "I guess not."

"Want me to read the card for you?" Sheryl volunteered.

"No thanks." Preston took up the square wrapped box and then peeled off the large envelope pasted to it. He opened it carefully.

Dear Son,

Happy Birthday! The thirteenth is a significant number you made it on the verge of manhood. I am proud of the boy you are. I am excited to see the man you will become, my first-born. I wish our lives were different, but I can't for the life of me wish you away from existence. Our lives are far from perfect, because of my actions I have created a less than ideal situation in your lives but I am happy that you were born. I love every one of my children with all I have, and I just want you to know Preston, that I love you. I have not always gotten the opportunity to show it, but I need for you to know. I'll always love you, and I will always be here for you when you need me.

With all my love,
Dad.

"You should save it." Sheryl's soft voice said closer to him than he thought she was. He hadn't heard her move. She was reading the note over his shoulder.

"I saved all of the things my father gave me when he died."

Preston looked up at her with tear-drenched eyes and then nodded. "I will."

"I baked you a cake." Miss Pam cleared her throat, "I was wondering if you want to invite anyone over later for a birthday party."

"Good idea," Fred said jovially. "I can take over a crate of sodas, some potato chips, and ice cream."

"I don't think so." Preston shook his head. "It's just not right."

"You cannot stop celebrating your birthday because of what happened." Miss Pam squinted her eyes and looked at him. "I won't let you."

"I have some balloons…blue, and green, your favorite colors," Sheryl said hopefully.

Those were her favorite colors, Preston wanted to point out. He only said he loved them because she did. Where Sheryl was concerned he had a severe case of hero worship.

The other boys trooped into the kitchen.

"What do you boys think?" Miss Pam said, "Preston's birthday party later?"

"Yes!" Jordan was the first to answer, "Can I invite Shawn and Cody?"

"Of course," Pam said, "any friends you would like to invite, Preston?"

Preston shrugged. "Not really. Maybe Leroy and Otis. I have my brothers. I don't want a crowd."

"This is from the five of us," Walter said slapping a fridge magnet in front of Preston. "I picked it out myself."

"I helped." Guy piped in.

"I just wrote the names at the back," Jordan grinned. "It's an endorsement of the sentiments."

Preston turned it over; there were six names, in order of age, written in Jordan's boxy cursive handwriting.

"Thank you." Preston read the front out loud. "Between brothers there should come no other, a bond for life forever stronger."

He stared at it, for a while and then looked up at his brothers one by one. "I like that. It is a code we should live by. I am going to put it on the fridge."

He got up and put it on the refrigerator door and then turned around and looked at his siblings. Everyone one of them, from Case the youngest with his mop of curly hair to Jordan the second oldest who looked so much like him.

He loved them all.

Maybe their coming together was not ideal, but they were together.

That was how he would view this day. He shrugged off the sadness without much effort.

****

Jordan fumbled in the dark trying to open the front door after Preston's party. Jackie had promised to turn on the veranda light. It was either she didn't remember, or he had forgotten to pay the bill.

He finally fit the key in the proper slot and searched for the hall light. The house lit up, and he sank in relief on the door after closing it. He had not ironed his school uniform for tomorrow. He didn't want to arrive at school looking unkempt.

He had a reputation to maintain. He did not want anybody concerned about him and then got it into their head that he shouldn't be living alone or that he needed adult supervision.

He was just fine by himself. His mother had ensured that he learned the basics while growing up. He could run the house and take care of himself quite fine. He had a schedule to ensure that he was efficient. He glanced at it now. The light bill was due in three days. He would have to pay it after school tomorrow, after track club training.

He had homework to do tonight too. He groaned it was English; he wasn't necessarily fond of the subject. He would iron his clothes first while he watched an evening program.

He pulled the iron board to the living room and set it up. The living room was neat; he had developed a latent neat streak that he could trace straight back to this time last year. The murder of his parents had affected him on deeper levels than anyone knew.

He missed them; sometimes it felt like a physical pain. He had been determined that today would not be a bad day because it was Preston's birthday but now he could feel the effects of it—the loneliness, the despair, the urge to cry.

It was strong while he was heading to Preston's house and even stronger when he found the gift earlier.

He wished that he could just talk to his father one more time, and see his mother's face one more time.

He put down the iron and curled up in the long settee in a

fetal position. Tears were running down his cheeks freely.

He didn't know how long he was frozen in that position. His mind flitting from scene to scene where he ran over the things his mother said, the things his father said, the places they went to, and the things they did together as a family.

He thought he was mistaken when he heard a knock on the front door until it got more insistent.

He jumped up quickly and looked at the clock. It was just past eight. He looked through the peephole. It was Shawn.

He opened the door quickly. He wouldn't want anybody else to see him so miserable, but since it was Shawn, it was okay.

She took one look at him and held up her overnight bag. "I told Jackie that somebody had to stay with you tonight."

He nodded and stepped back closing the door behind her.

"What were you doing, apart from crying?" Shawn asked putting her bag down.

"Oh, your uniform. I'll do it."

Jordan sat back down on the settee. "I was just thinking about them."

"I know." Shawn tilted her head to one side and pushed her hand into her baggy shorts. "I saw you trying today to be upbeat and positive, and I literally ached for you."

Jordan looked at her familiar face. She had changed this year. Her face was angling out, smoothing out into a definitely feminine look.

Shawn was pretty. Like really pretty. He didn't know why he hadn't seen it before. She had warm brown skin, a shade or two darker than his, brown eyes that were the exact shade of his mother's liquid vanilla, a short pointy little nose that gave her an inquisitive air and her lips...

He stared at them for longer than he should. They were red.

How had he ever thought Shawn was a boy?

Despite her baggy clothes, he could see her breasts a fascinating set of arrivals that were easily seen when she was wearing her new school uniform.

Shawn looked at him annoyed. "You want to talk to me about it?"

"About what?" Jordan frowned.

"Your feelings. The reason you couldn't finish ironing. The reason you were curled up in the settee crying."

"No er," Jordan stammered, "I ah..."

Shawn looked at him strangely. "I am going to iron your khakis. I must say I miss mine. I hate wearing girl's uniform. You are acting weird."

"Sorry." Jordan dragged his mind from Shawn's new and unexpected allure. It had to be the day and what it signified. It was making him think things. Things he shouldn't.

"We can do the English homework together," Shawn said plugging in the iron.

"Yes." Jordan exhaled.

"Preston's party was great, wasn't it?" Shawn continued. "He is such a sweet person. You know I think I like him. There is something about him. Maybe it's the fact that he is getting taller or cuter."

"What?" Jordan sat up straighter on the settee. "Say that again?"

"I am just saying." Shawn bit her lip. "He's cute."

"You like boys?" The shock in Jordan's voice reverberated in the air.

"Of course I like boys," Shawn said offended. "I am not a lesbian."

"That's not what I mean, I just..." Jordan looked at her again, "Preston though?"

"Why not?" Shawn asked. "He is really nice."

Jordan shook his head. "No. Just no."

"I know right? At first, when I thought about it I was like, no way! What is going on in my head?" Shawn shrugged. "I told Jackie about my new interest, and she was saying that maybe I am going to be attracted to quieter boys you know... the strong silent types.

"No, I don't know." Jordan felt his head throb. "You can't be attracted to Preston."

"I know," Shawn smirked. "I am waiting for it to pass. After all, if I can be attracted to Preston, I could be attracted to you, the two of you look alike, and if that happened, it would be crazy, sort of like incest."

Jordan rubbed his temples rigorously. "Yeah, that would be crazy."

"So who do you like?" Shawn asked looking at him knowingly. "I know you must like somebody."

"I don't," Jordan said defensively.

"I thought we told each other everything," Shawn said accusation rife in her voice.

"We do." Jordan shrugged, "I just don't like anybody right now."

"Liar," Shawn muttered. "I sense that you like someone. You better tell me, or I'll tickle it out of you."

Jordan looked at her in consternation. He couldn't tell her the truth. He couldn't tell her that he had developed an alarming fascination with her. She was right. It would be like incest.

"Talk." Shawn held up the iron and made a mock tough face at him.

"I like Summer," Jordan said thinking of the first name that came to his head. Summer B. Fallon, everybody liked her. She had quite an admiration society at the school.

Shawn snorted. "Every boy likes Summer. She has long

hair and fair skin. Her smile pisses me off. It's too wide, and she does it too much."

Jordan chuckled. "You sound jealous."

"Maybe." Shawn snorted. "What is it about long hair that boys find so exciting. Maybe I should grow mine see what all the fuss is about."

Jordan declined to respond. Summer didn't hold a candle to Shawn facially, with or without long hair.

He had to stop thinking like this, but he was afraid that now that it was in his head it wasn't going to stop.

Chapter Fourteen

I think the four of you should work at the supermarket for the next few months. Fred said to Preston, Jordan, Walter, and Guy.

They had been around the table planning what they were going to do for the summer. Preston was feeling especially nonchalant about the holidays. He was mostly listening to his brothers, especially Jordan rave about his plans to be a rafting operator at the Blue Lagoon.

Jordan was salivating at the thought. Walter wanted in on it and was offering to help build the bamboo rafts. Guy was already spending the tourist dollars they would collect from the business.

Fred mercifully suggested working at the supermarket.

Preston was the first to nod. "Yes!"

"No!" Jordan looked aghast. "That's boring!"

"It is your business," Fred retorted, "you boys should take an interest in it."

"But...rafting," Jordan said weakly.

"What's the pay?" Walter asked, "Is it anything near what we would get from our rafting venture?"

"I have no clue." Fred frowned. "I am not even sure that you would have made any money from your rafting venture. All I am saying, boys, is this, you are the owners of Wiley Groceries, you should take an interest in this business. I might not always be around."

"Where are you going?" Preston asked fearfully.

"I have no plans to go anywhere, yet." Fred looked at them frankly. "Anything can happen in this life. You boys had a raw deal handed to you with your parents and stuff, but you have a legacy. And it is time you paid some attention to it."

"I wish one of you older boys would be interested."

"I want to be a farmer." Guy shrugged, "I don't want to work in a supermarket."

"I want to be either a pharmacist or a doctor, whichever pays more," Walter said raising an eyebrow, "and takes less time at school."

"I think I want to design houses," Jordan said contemplatively, "or maybe just be a rafter."

Fred looked at Preston. "And you?"

"I want to work at the supermarket," Preston said frankly. "I want to expand too, move out of Portland and into the rest of Jamaica."

Fred heaved a sigh. "Thank God one of you wants to work at the family business and even expand it. It still doesn't make a difference though whether in the future you want to be a pharmacist, a farmer or an architect.

"You are all coming to work full time this summer and part-time the rest of the year. It will build character and responsibility. You all will be working your own wages. After you start, there will be no lunch money or pocket money from me. Only Saint and Case will be getting pocket money. From now on, you are all working men."

Walter groaned. "Really?"

"Child labor," Guy said dispassionately.

Fred laughed. "I will put each of you in every area, warehouse, cashier, purchasing, administration. That is how old man Riddley started your father. When I am done with you, you should be able to run your business quite ably."

"You sure, you okay?" Preston asked Fred.

"Of course." Fred nodded. "I am fine."

"You not tired of us and planning to leave?" Preston asked the question a kernel of panic hitting him in the chest.

"I promised you I would be here for you until you are an adult," Fred said firmly. "Stop worrying, Preston. "

He looked at the rest of the boys. "You have a week's holiday. Report to work July 5th…dress code, blue jeans and white t-shirt."

Fred got up from the table. "Work starts at eight, ends at four. You have an hour lunch break. You get your pay every two weeks. You will be treated just the same as everyone else. No more no less."

Miss Pam came into the kitchen with a basket of clothes at her side. "You laying down the law, Fred?"

"Oh yes." Fred nodded.

"July the fifth is my birthday," Jordan muttered.

"Welcome to the real world." Fred snorted. "I work on my birthday every year."

"Likewise." Miss Pam sniffed. "Last year I even forgot about it."

"I am a part of the real world." Jordan got up. "I live alone, I wash my own clothes, and pay my bills."

Then he snapped his fingers. "Say, can Shawn come and work with us this summer?"

"That would be great!" Preston said quickly. He liked hanging with Shawn. She was the coolest girl in the world. He could see why Jordan loved her company so much.

Jordan looked at him sharply when he said that and wondered why he did.

"Sure, why not?" Fred said. "If she wants to work, she's welcomed."

"And Sheryl," Preston looked at Miss Pam and then back at Fred, "can she come too?"

"Actually, Sheryl asked to work at the supermarket which gave me the idea..." Fred said sheepishly. "It was a nudge in the right direction."

"That's my girl." Miss Pam looked at them. "She knows the value of hard work and I didn't even suggest it to her. Imagine that, as I said she is destined for greatness."

****

It was the turning point, that summer. He had hit puberty with a vengeance. He had hair growing in places where he never had it before, his armpit his pubic area; even his face had a strand or two.

He thought about Sheryl often, and sometimes Shawn, and he had wet dreams, like twice in one night and he had a lurid fascination with breasts, big ones, small ones. Sheryl's or Shawn's, breasts were more fascinating than learning the inner workings of the supermarket business.

It was driving him slightly crazy, his fascination. Added to that his voice was croaky. He knew he would be kicked off the school choir when they went back to school and he felt as if he smelled.

He liked Miss Pam, but he couldn't talk to her about the new developments. He wasn't comfortable talking to Fred or

Pastor Tate either. Maybe if he ignored it, it would go away. But he couldn't.

By the second week in August he was having trouble looking both Shawn and Sheryl in the eye. He figured they knew his fantasies about them and all of a sudden he was getting nervous around them.

Jordan didn't seem to have that problem. They were just eight weeks apart in age, why on earth was Jordan normal, and he wasn't?

They were outwardly developing the same. Jordan was on the same height as he was. His voice was also wonky and getting deeper. He was getting broader in the shoulder area too, so how was it that Jordan seemed so unfazed by the new changes and he always smelled good.

Preston fretted about it for weeks. He wanted to ask Jordan what he was doing and how he was dealing with it but he never really got the chance. Jordan was never really alone. Shawn was always with him like a shadow. The last thing Preston wanted was for Shawn to know what he was thinking.

They had a routine. The six of them went to work every day. Sheryl had a fixed job as a cashier. Shawn was placed in the Purchasing office where she had a whole pile of papers to file. The boys were shunted from one area of the operation to the next with Fred watching over them keenly to see where they excelled.

After a few weeks, it was clear that Preston did very well with the administration, sometimes making suggestions to improve certain areas that had Fred nodding in approval.

Jordan had yet to find his niche. He hated the office and preferred the warehouse area where he processed orders when they came in. And he took his lunch by the Folly Ruins as soon as the clock struck twelve, usually with Shawn in tow.

To get him alone, Preston had to tell Shawn that he wanted to spend lunchtime with his brother alone.

"Why?" Shawn grinned at him. It was near midday. Preston had to act fast.

Shawn had the prettiest, smoothest skin he had ever seen. No one else was as smooth and blemish-free as Shawn. She always had her hair pulled back in a ponytail, and it emphasized her cheekbones.

Goodness, had she always been that pretty?

"Preston?" Shawn snapped her fingers in front of his face.

"Yes er well, I need to talk to him about boy stuff." Preston cleared his throat. "Man to man, no girls allowed kind of thing."

"Okay." Shawn shrugged. "I guess I could find Sheryl and see what she is doing."

"Thank you," Preston mumbled and stepped back out of the room.

Shawn shook her head and continued with her work.

Preston had to pause and look at her one last time before leaving, almost getting caught.

****

They crossed the road and headed for Folly Island where the ruins of the Roman Style villa sat in neglect near the sea. The place was just called Folly Great House by everyone. It looked like it would have been a gorgeous house if most of the upstairs hadn't collapsed.

Jordan made his way over the wind-ravaged grass, and Preston followed him. Lunch for him was a sandwich from the supermarket deli and a box drink with a smiling orange at the side.

"Why do you like over here so much?" He followed Jordan

as they sat on the edge of a floor that overlooked the sea and Monkey Island.

"It's quiet, and it gives me time to think." Jordan looked at him curiously. "Have you ever been over here?"

"Only once." Preston shrugged. "Why do you need time to think? You live alone, and you are always over here with Shawn anyway."

Jordan bit into his sandwich and didn't answer.

"What do you want to talk to me about?" He turned to Preston.

"Puberty." Preston looked down at his sandwich and then up at Jordan sheepishly. "I've been going through some stuff, and I thought it would be good to hear if I am normal."

Jordan inhaled and then looked at Preston. "You do know you are the older one of the two of us?"

"Yeah, so?" Preston growled, "when has that ever been a problem for you. You act like the older one anyway. You are more worldly than me."

"That's true, and this is awkward," Jordan said folding his sandwich wrapper over and over again.

"I know, but we have four other brothers for you to give the talk to so this is practice." Preston sighed. "Why is it that you smell so good?"

"I use Dad's perfume." Jordan shrugged. "He bought them in bulk. CK for men. I've been in his stash. He told us once that it is always good to smell good. People liked that. I also use a lot of roll on. And I never go to bed without showering."

"Oh," Preston frowned. "I don't...I must buy some roll on."

Jordan nodded. "Aunt Sharla sent a whole pack of the thing a couple of months ago. I can give you some of mine."

"Thanks." Preston nodded. "I er have you ever, I mean... had er..."

"Wet dreams." Jordan sighed. "Had my first one when I was eleven. Both Mom and Dad said it was normal I had nothing to be ashamed about etcetera."

Preston giggled. "Eleven?"

"What can I say?" Jordan took a sip of his drink. "Dad said he was my age when he started getting them too. He also said my penis size was normal I asked."

Preston gasped. "What?"

"Yup, I used to talk about stuff like that with him." Jordan inhaled, "I miss him so much. I remember thinking how cringey it was to be talking to him about man stuff. That's what he used to call our talks. Now I would do anything for just one more talk."

"I didn't have that kind of relationship with him."

"That means you never got the sex talk?" Jordan looked at Preston quizzically. "I got it the night before my first day of high school."

"Wow. No, I didn't." Preston shook his head. "With Dad and I, it was hi, how are you? Good. Okay then. Well, that was until he moved out. In many ways, he lived with us, but I never got much of him."

"It wasn't his fault. Dad was very hands on." Jordan sighed. "I wish I could have seen him with our little sister. She would have made things different."

"Yep." Preston sighed. "She would have. We would have a sister."

"I want to be like Dad if I have kids. He was an excellent father." Jordan sighed. "A good person over all."

"I never got the chance to..." Preston felt his voice choking up. "I wish I knew him better. I guess I will have to learn to be a good father."

"Or call me." Jordan grinned at him. "Or we come over to Folly and have a heart to heart and hash out our fatherly struggles."

"Yeah." Preston cleared his throat. "It's good to know I am not a freak, though. Should have talked to you a long time ago. Do you think about breasts constantly?"

"Yes." Jordan nodded. "Every day, every hour."

Preston laughed in relief. "Okay. But you are not as awkward with it as I am."

"My best friend is a girl." Jordan shrugged. "She has them. She hates them. She complains about them all the time."

"Yeah, I noticed that she has them." Preston inhaled. "I can't look Shawn or Sheryl in the face anymore."

"You'd better..." Jordan looked at him fiercely. "I don't know about Sheryl, but you look Shawn in the face!"

"Okay." Preston held up his hand. "I hear you."

"She is off limits!" Jordan said fiercely.

Preston nodded. " It's as though she just blossomed into someone else overnight like she is no longer a dude like she did some surgery or something."

"I know." Jordan sighed. "If my mother was alive she would say I told you so. Shawn is now an honest to goodness girl."

"Honest to goodness girl," Preston repeated.

"Dad was sexually active at fourteen." Jordan looked at Preston. "That's our age."

"He was?" Preston widened his eyes. "How would you know this?"

"He told me." Jordan sighed, "I told you I got the talk and Dad didn't hold back anything."

Preston nodded. "So?"

"So we are not going to be like him. He warned me not to be." Jordan looked at Preston. "We are going to be different. My mom got pregnant at fifteen and lost the baby. She and Dad were living in poverty."

"That I know." Preston snorted. "That's why Dad took the deal with my grandfather and why I am even here. He married for money but still kept his true love."

"We can have a better story," Jordan said determination lacing his voice. "Just remember that when the hormones kick in."

Preston chuckled. "Sounds like you have it all under control, old man."

"Nope." Jordan stood up and stretched. "But whenever I think of April 26, 1998, it's good enough to keep me in check. I know I can't live the kind of mix up life our parents did. I want to be different."

Preston nodded, his eyes cloudy. "I agree. Self-control. Avoid love triangles. Avoid crazy women. Avoid drama."

"And stay away from Shawn," Jordan said abruptly. "She is off limits."

"Heard you the first time," Preston muttered, "loud and clear."

Chapter Fifteen

"**S**hawn Marie Mason reporting for drudgery," Shawn smirked at Jackie as soon as she reached the hair salon. Jackie had pleaded with her to come and help out because she was short staffed.

Being around women and their chatter ranked very high on the list of things she hated. She would have preferred to be hanging out with Jordan at their swimming spot by the Blue Lagoon.

It was a public holiday for mercy's sake. Heroes Day. Jackie and her clients had no respect for the heroes.

To make matters worse, she had been confined to the house yesterday because of homework, and today she had to work at the salon and tomorrow it would be something else. Since the summer holiday when she worked at the supermarket and started seeing her period Jackie had turned into a jailer.

She couldn't play with the boys at will anymore. She couldn't sleep over at Jordan's either and Jackie, and her father had conspired to buy her new girly clothes. Her freedom was being curtailed slowly and surely.

"Good, you are here." Jackie grinned at her over the lady's hair she was washing.

"As if I had a choice." Shawn pouted. "You threatened me."

"Don't let the customers hear that," Jackie said unrepentantly "they are accustomed to willing service with a smile."

The ladies who were patiently waiting their turn laughed. Jackie's assistant, Shay, who was lathering relaxer on a customer's hair, pointed to a hamper of towels.

"First job, get those clean. The washing machine is at the back…line dry them it's a beautiful sunny day, but we are running out, so hurry."

"Hello to you too Shay." Shawn stuck her tongue out at Shay who had her hair coifed in red braids, which matched her red lipstick almost perfectly.

Jackie cleared her throat. "No juvenile behavior, Missy."

"Yes mother," Shawn said cheekily. She had stopped calling Jackie mom or mommy or any of those terms when she was about six. Jackie had hated it then, but she had gotten used to it. When Shawn called her mother, she knew Shawn was mocking her.

"I have no idea where I got you from," Jackie muttered. "You are so different from other girls. "

"For a time she wasn't even a girl." Shay snorted. "You encouraged it, Jackie."

"I might have," Jackie shrugged, "but I was glad because she was not interested in boys or stuff like that. I knew one day she would grow out of the tomboy stage."

"I am not out of any stage," Shawn muttered. "I am still a tomboy!"

"No, you are not." Jackie shook her head, "you like boys now, and I am not giving you an opportunity to make me a grandmother before I am ready. You are going to be a virgin on your wedding night. You are going to live a circumspect and different life from me."

"Tell her, Jackie." Shay pointed at the hamper. "Come, miss, get cracking! We are seriously running out of towels."

Shawn gave Shay the evil eye and headed to the back veranda where there was a washing machine and dryer. She loaded it following the instructions on the wall and then sat down on a stool facing Jordan's section of the house.

A security grill separated the verandas, and a flowerbed spanned the expanse between the two spaces.

Guy was using it as his little farming project. It had tomatoes and green peppers and what looked like a melon vine.

Jordan complained that since Guy lived elsewhere, he was the one who had to take care of his garden.

Shawn sighed, she wished Jordan was home, at least he would make her day more bearable, but it was wishful thinking. Jordan would not be at home when he didn't have to. He was like her; he liked to be out in the vast spaces exploring. Hunting for fruits, climbing trees, swimming. Portland was the perfect place to live for those kinds of endeavors.

Instead, she was stuck because girls did not have that kind of freedom. All of a sudden since she had gained breasts and had her period she had to act a certain way and dress a certain way. Jackie had even forbidden her to cut her hair again.

Even though she had been toying with the thought of growing it out and seeing what the big deal was. She just didn't like that Jackie had ordered her not to cut it.

It was her hair.

She massaged it a bit more out of boredom than anything else; it was now a little past her neck in a mass of thick corkscrew curls, which she kept pinned up all the time except for today. She needed to get it washed when Jackie had no customers left.

Jackie loved her hair and kept telling her how lucky she was that her curls were springy and shiny.

She had no idea if it was just Jackie's propaganda to get her to grow it out or if she was genuinely envious of her curls.

She had no idea why hair was such a big deal. Maybe if she had spent more time with the girls at school, she would know.

The only girl she spent extra time with was Sheryl, and all she spoke about was books and college and grades and lately church. Sheryl was little miss prim and proper before church; now she was a holy prim and proper. If she didn't go to church one Sabbath, Sheryl would dutifully recite to her Pastor Tate's sermons like a parrot.

It was faintly disturbing being in her presence these days, Shawn concluded because she was the opposite of prim and she and proper and had only a passing acquaintance with the church and Bible and all of that holy jazz.

The last time she had stepped into a church was about six weeks ago when Jordan had insisted that she go for a children's Sabbath where the children put on the service. She had to admit it had been different and intriguing.

Sheryl though was a constant staple there. Shawn had all but given up on them being closer. She was the only girl candidate in her opinion; all the other girls at school were too girly.

She wished there was a girl that could take the place of Jordan—best friend, listening board, knew her inside out. But there was no one, and according to society, their relationship had to cease and proper bounds be placed upon it because she was getting older.

It was a bunch of poop and society only thought that way because they were rotten perverts.

She hopped off the stool at the same time that the back door to Jordan's side opened. He was in jeans shorts that were threadbare and faded and an equally ratty t-shirt that looked as if he had outgrown it. He had gotten taller and more muscular. He was growing up. She couldn't take him down in a fight anymore.

He yawned and stretched. He hadn't seen her yet.

Shawn swallowed. Her heart was doing the fast throbs that it had started doing around Jordan. Her throat was suddenly dry.

Society wasn't the pervert. She was.

Things were not the same between her and her beloved Jordy. She had a huge, gigantic crush on him that would not quit. She had tried transference a year ago; pretending that she liked Preston when it was really him she liked but it hadn't worked. Jordan was simply Jordan, different, earthy, and cuter than Preston in her opinion with his limpid brown eyes and his honey brown complexion.

Jordan looked up at the same time that she made to move away and he didn't say a word.

No hi. No, come on over. No, let's get out of here.

They were standing and looking at each other like they were combatants.

Things were not the same between them; lately, it was obvious, and it hurt.

Jordan moved his head to one side and folded his arm. "You look different with your hair out."

"Oh," Shawn touched her hair. "I didn't realize."

"Almost didn't recognize you," Jordan said pointing to her dress.

"My father sent it." Shawn hissed. "He sent a whole barrel of dresses and shoes with heels. No sneakers or t-shirts or baggy jeans."

Jordan chuckled. "I can see how that would rattle you."

"I thought you would be at the beach now," Shawn said wistfully. "I didn't know you'd be home."

"A big part of going to the beach is hanging with you." Jordan came closer to the grill. "You weren't available, and Preston is helping Sheryl with some project or the other. Miss Glenda took the four younger boys to Kingston for the half term."

Shawn felt warmth envelop her at his confession. He didn't feel like going without her. That was something; at least he still loved her company.

"So what are you doing today then?" she pressed her face on the grill.

"Reading," Jordan smirked. "Well, actually finishing up a book that Guy loaned to me. He is so excited about it. It's called the Alchemist. It's about a boy who was on a journey to find his personal legend."

"What's that?" Shawn frowned.

"Personal legend is your true purpose in life." Jordan scratched his head. "I guess you could call it your life's spiritual purpose. It's living your passion, what you were made for. According to the author, everybody is born knowing what their purpose is; you just have to find it. It's good stuff. I will buy you a copy for your birthday because this copy is going to Preston after I am done."

"You could have made it a surprise," Shawn muttered. "I like surprises."

"I know." Jordan grinned. "You are so predictable."

****

Her birthday, November 8. She was finally fourteen. Jackie was so excited it was irritating. Shawn watched as her mother flitted to and from her room like an excited dog on steroids.

Only thing left was for her to pant and wag a tail.

"Aren't you going to get dressed?" Jackie asked looking at the clock.

"Why should I? It's just Dad, and it's a Sunday," Shawn said laconically. "I see him three times for the year. He calls here constantly. I don't get why you are so happy."

Jackie did not pay her any mind. She spun around their tiny house as if she forgot something which was impossible since Jackie had been cleaning and scrubbing the two bedroom ranch style house like a mad woman since last Thursday. She had even gotten the lawn cut and had the trees trimmed and repainted the walls around the quarter acre property.

Shawn used to think that her mother's over excitement was because of her birthday, but she had long since given up on that idea.

Her mother went into a tizzy because her father, Dan Mason, was coming to Jamaica. He came back for her birthday every year, and he usually stayed a month. He slept in her mother's room, and he ran the house like he was always there. Her mother deferred to him like a pseudo-wife willing to do whatever he bid.

When he came in February with his wife Eden and their twins, they stayed at Frenchman's Cove Hotel.

At that time he only visited them at night, and he left in the wee hours of the morning. If perchance, he requested that Shawn visited with Eden and the twins, he always warned her, not to tell them, that he had seen her the night before.

She had kept her mouth shut because she did not talk much when she was around Eden.

Eden was kind to her; she was an English lady with long blonde hair, green eyes, and creamy looking skin. Eden was super caring; you could see it when she was around her children Sage and Athena.

Shawn just wasn't comfortable with her or with her brother and sister either. They were strangers who she saw once a year, for a few days at a time, maybe that would change, the twins were around seven now.

Until she had met the twins and Eden, Shawn had not realized that her family was as screwed up as it was.

It was kind of like Jordan's but without the fireworks. Her mother was the mistress, her father's port of call when he was in Jamaica. When he was here, he was here. And he didn't miss a beat with running the place when he was away.

Jackie liked the status quo. It wasn't conventional, but it worked for her. That was probably why she and Hannah had been such good friends. They had similar arrangements except Hannah's arrangement had gotten her killed.

Shawn steepled her hands under her chin.

"What are you looking so thoughtful about?" Jackie asked walking into the living room with a potted plant and proceeded to fix it just right to make a good impression.

Shawn rolled her eyes. "I was thinking that you are not that bad looking."

"Thank you, Shawn Marie," Jackie looked around at her. "What made you say that?"

"You should get a man of your own and stop fooling around with Dad."

"Our situation is handled." Jackie looked at her angrily. "You are crossing the line here Shawn."

"No, I am not." Shawn shook her head. "Don't you worry that one day Eden will get mad and come to the shop and shoot you just like Jennifer did to Hannah?"

"Stop the madness, child!" Jackie growled. "Eden doesn't know about your dad and me, as far as she knows it was over between us years ago. He only married her for the citizenship."

"And he stayed because..." Shawn raised an eyebrow.

"Conversation over!" Jackie said sharply. "I am not discussing this with you."

"But when will you discuss it?" Shawn asked irritated. "It is my life too."

"This is between the adults." Jackie fixed her plant and stood back and admired it. She looked at Shawn dispassionately. "Last I checked you were still just fourteen. You have a couple of years left before you even understand half of the things I go through to be comfortable in this life."

Shawn smirked. "Do you love my Dad?"

"Of course I love Dan." Jackie snapped. "Would I love him even more if he were here and belonged to us exclusively? I am not so sure. I like the fact that I see him once or twice a year. I like my weekly Western Union money transfers. I like my freedom to be who I am without any man underfoot running my life. I do it for a month; Eden gets him for the year. He takes care of us. I am fine. Questions over. Go get ready for your Dad and leave your hair out so that he can see how it is growing."

Shawn got up reluctantly. "I think you can do better than this, Jackie."

"And I think, having a fourteen-year-old philosopher around is getting on my last nerve!" Jackie mumbled. "I have a mind, not to give you your birthday gift."

****

Shawn finally got a break from her mother and father in the evening. Her dad had turned on his turntable and was playing Skeeter Davis Gospel songs; she couldn't escape the house fast enough.

She knew when that album finished he would put in his Charlie Pride and Jim Reeves. He was punishing her, and it was her birthday. No, she couldn't—wouldn't appreciate old gospel music and she wouldn't be forced to either.

She headed to Jordan's as soon as she finished the elaborate dinner Jackie had prepared. She had some in a container for Jordan: baked chicken, curried goat, oxtail, rice and peas and potato salad. Her mother had cooked as if she was preparing for an army.

She even had ice cream and cake. She would have to wait until the food settled before she could attempt dessert and only if her father finished with his old gospel songs.

Jordan was sitting on the veranda when she got there. He had company: Sheryl and Preston.

To her knowledge, it was the first time Miss Prim and Prissy Sheryl was coming to their end of the neighborhood. Miss Pam usually had Sheryl on a tight leash—*Her daughter who would one day rule the world.* Shawn thought snarkily.

Maybe she was just bitter because Sheryl was smart and bright and her mother had grand ambitions for her.

Jackie's only ambition for Shawn was that she graduate from school without getting pregnant.

"Hey, guys." Shawn greeted them cheerfully.

"Shawn!" Jordan jumped up when she came toward him. "I see that you have food."

"Lots of it." Shawn grinned, "Jackie cooked for an army

though it was only the three of us."

"We took food for Jordan's Sunday dinner already," Sheryl said. "He just ate."

"I am a growing boy," Jordan opened the container and inhaled. "Thank you, Shawn. This smells like heaven."

Shawn giggled. And then turned to Sheryl who was in a pretty dress with a matching headband around her hair. "What brings you to our neck of the woods?"

"Church program," Sheryl said. "I thought I would invite Jordan along."

Preston nodded. "It's not until five. Maybe you can come, Shawn."

"Do they sing Skeeter Davis kind of songs?" Shawn asked wearily.

"No." Sheryl frowned. "What's wrong with Skeeter Davis, I love her songs. My dad used to play them a lot I miss him so much. When I hear them, I think about him."

Shawn frowned. "To each his own. My situation is vastly different. My dad murders me with it when he is here."

Jordan started eating and then paused. "I will go if you go, Shawn. Remember you liked the service a couple of weeks ago?"

"Yep, I remember." Shawn made a face, "but one old lady told me not to wear pants to church. I had no idea that one requirement to going to heaven was wearing a dress."

"It's just the dress code." Preston grinned, "Everybody has a dress code, even schools. Stop nitpicking. You are in a dress; you will fit in just fine."

Shawn groaned. She wished she wasn't wearing one, but Jackie had turned into an evil fiend and burned her baggiest pants and looser t-shirts. And she had insisted that Shawn wear a dress for her birthday. It was a pretty jeans dress that was not too tight or particular shape enhancing but it was still a dress.

"You look pretty," Jordan said and then followed it up with one of his smiles. The one that had the power to melt her heart.

"It is just the one time, and Sheryl here is going to sing. You know I can't go anywhere without you."

"Are we walking?" Shawn asked looking at Sheryl.

"No," Sheryl shook her head. "Preston and I rode here."

"Oh, then maybe I should go for my bicycle," Shawn said. "By the time I get back, Jordan should be done eating."

****

The trip back to her house was less than three minutes. Her parents were locked up in their room. *Probably couldn't wait until she left the house to do the dirty*, Shawn thought resentfully. How could they have sex to Skeeter Davis music was a mystery, somehow the two didn't seem to work well together.

Do you know my Jesus? Do you know my friend? Have you heard he loves you and that he will abide till the end...

The music blared all the way down to the end of the street.

She got her bicycle, cursing the fact that she had to wear a dress and then realized that it wasn't that bad.

It was a perfect day. The evening sun had a golden hue. It bathed everything in a benevolent light. The breeze was cool on her face as she rode to Jordan's place. Jordan had called her pretty.

He had never given her such a compliment before. Something had shifted. She could feel it between them, and she wasn't sure that she liked it too much. She didn't dislike it, but she hated change. Jackie was right. Things get complicated when you get older.

When she reached the house Sheryl and Preston were standing near their bicycles; Jordan was dressed in jeans and a white shirt.

"That's some record." Shawn grinned at him.

"Just changed my shirt." Jordan shrugged. "Let's go. I have a present for you when you get back."

"It's your birthday?" Preston asked Shawn.

"Yup. I was hatched around this time of the year." Shawn giggled.

"I could have gotten you a present or something," Preston muttered. "Sorry."

"No problem." Shawn got on her bike. "Once Jordan doesn't forget I am fine."

"You two are official now?" Sheryl asked looking at the two of them.

"Officially what?" Jordan got on his bicycle and then rode through the gate.

Shawn frowned grimly at Sheryl. "Jordan is my best friend. No more crazy talk about being a couple."

"Sorry," Sheryl mumbled.

"So, you two official then, that's why you want company?" Shawn asked looking between Sheryl and Preston.

"Nah," Preston said sheepishly and got on his bike.

"My mother would kill me," Sheryl said to Shawn wistfully. "You know she has high hopes for me. I can have no boyfriends, not even Preston. We live in the same house, that would be virtually a recipe for disaster."

Shawn nodded. "Yep."

"But I like him." Sheryl sighed and fluttered her thick eyelashes at Shawn. "You understand what I am saying?"

Shawn considered her for a moment. It was the first time she could remember feeling like Sheryl was human.

"I get you."

"And he is so cute. He is past cute."

Shawn chuckled. "Yeah. I hear you. He looks like Jordan."

"Yep." Sheryl got on her bicycle. "Both of them are delicious."

"Delicious?" Shawn snorted. You make them sound like food."

"But they are." Sheryl rode ahead of her and then looked back. "Do not tell anybody I said any of that."

"I wouldn't dare, Miss Prissy." Shawn smiled and gave her a thumbs up. Unfortunately, she wasn't going to keep her promise she would have to tell Jordan. She told him everything.

He would probably find it funny that Sheryl found him delicious.

The boys were waiting for them at the intersection of the main road.

They had the road mostly to themselves. They rode up towards San San and past the various hotels and guesthouses on that strip of road. They passed a few cyclists, most of them were decked out in helmets and colorful cycling gear.

They waved and hollered to them as they passed.

"I love this!" Sheryl sped past Shawn, Jordan, and Preston. "I may be a town girl, but I am the boss on a bicycle."

"Be careful!" Shawn shouted.

"You are just jealous that I am better at this than you." Sheryl looked back and stuck out her tongue. "I can race like the wind!"

"No, you are not the boss at this," Preston said racing past Sheryl with no effort.

"That's my boy," Jordan said easily.

Shawn laughed. "If we all showed her that she is still a town girl, she'd get left behind."

"I heard that!" Sheryl squealed indignantly. And I am

going to teach you..."

She never got to finish her sentence. A Toyota Crown whipped around the corner with Mrs. Wren at the wheel. She was a German retiree who was too old to be at the wheel.

She was also partially blind in one eye and didn't see them; she didn't utilize her car horn when she came around the corner.

She passed perilously close to Preston who veered out of the road in time, but she clipped Sheryl's bicycle sending her flying over the handle and into the ravine below.

Chapter Sixteen

The New Year was bittersweet for Preston. He didn't feel much like celebrating it. There was something about spending it at the hospital that made things a little depressing. Sheryl was drifting in and out of consciousness, and the doctors had called Miss Pam excitedly. It seemed as if she was finally fully aware of her surroundings.

They had all piled in the vehicle with Fred in the hopes of seeing her. She wasn't allowed visitors for the past six weeks except for Miss Pam.

He heard that it had been touch and go for a while. One of her legs was broken, and an arm and a couple of her ribs were fractured, but the doctors were more worried about her brain.

She had lost consciousness on impact and had woken up and then slipped into unconsciousness again, only coming back for a few minutes every day and usually, she didn't recognize Miss Pam.

Sheryl's hospitalization put a damper on Preston's mood all through November and the Christmas holiday. He didn't have much time to grieve. He had to work after school and had to drop his extracurricular activities because it was the busiest time of the year at the supermarket and Fred needed the help.

All the boys even eight-year-old Case had worked hard this holiday. In addition to that, they had to pick up the slack at home because Miss Pam was not really present. They had told her to stop making dinner for the time being. She was putting sugar for salt and burning things. She was too distracted to be in the kitchen.

He felt exhausted. Today he was supposed to be in bed snoozing. Tomorrow, he, Walter and Guy had two acres of lawn to cut. They had gotten rid of the gardener, according to Fred they had a slight cash flow problem but it was nothing to worry about the Christmas season would take care of it.

Preston still worried though. He had never heard his parents speak of having a cash flow problem when they were alive. He had always thought that the supermarket would be in the black forever.

He closed his eyes, and Fred sat beside him with a grunt. "Why are they taking so long?"

"I don't know," Preston murmured. "Maybe it's good news."

Miss Pam came back into the waiting room with a broad smile on her face. "Thanks to Jesus, my savior my deliverer my keeper, my help in times past, my help in times to come!"

Fred cleared his throat and started wiggling in his chair. He wasn't a religious man, and he got very uncomfortable when people expressed their Godly affection. "Is Sheryl okay?"

"Yes, she is," Miss Pam said fervently. "I mean she woke up and she recognized me. She remembers the accident. She remembers everything.

"The doctors say they will have a specialist come in and test for neurological damage, but they doubt anything is wrong."

Miss Pam sat in a seat across from them. "My Sheryl is asking about school and some assignment she had to complete but didn't get the chance to. I doubt she has any damages. I tell you, God is good!"

"Amen." Fred nodded.

Preston grinned at Fred's sharp amen, but he was feeling almost as happy as Miss Pam. Hearing that Sheryl was not showing signs of mental trauma was more than good news.

"Can we see her?" he couldn't take the eagerness from his voice.

"Not today," Miss Pam sighed, "tomorrow though. The doctor said she could be out by the end of this week. I will take care of her at home."

"And is Mrs. Wren's son still going to foot the bill?" Fred murmured.

"Oh yes." Miss Pam nodded vigorously. "He said he will pay her hospital and recovery fees and that I have nothing to worry about."

"They are rich," Fred said. "You should sue them. His mother was driving without a license. It's an open and shut case."

"You know what the Lord told me, Fred. He said, don't sue her. He said forgive, and I will heal Sheryl." Miss Pam sighed, "I am just happy that my baby is alive and well and not damaged in the head. Praise God!"

"The Lord said that? How do you even..." Fred opened his mouth to argue and then shut it back. "Okay, fine. We can't argue with the 'Lord'."

"I don't expect you to understand." Miss Pam got up. "I

expect ridicule but God saved Sheryl, and I am keeping my end of the bargain. I also promised God that as soon as I can, I would go back to him. For years I blamed God for taking Michael, my husband. I blamed him, I turned my back on him, but I should not have. God giveth and he taketh away. He is God, who am I to question his plans."

Fred sighed heavily; he looked like he wanted to be anywhere but here with Miss Pam. "You guys ready?"

"Sure." Preston jumped up. "I'll go get the others."

His brothers were on the hospital porch looking out at the sea. Case was curled up in a chair asleep, and Guy was reading How To Win Friends and Influence People by Dale Carnegie.

Preston looked at the title and shook his head. After Guy finished reading his books, he gave it to them and insisted that they read it.

"Is it any good?" He asked.

Guy looked up from his book and grinned. "Oh yes, it is. Didn't you like the Alchemist?"

"Yes." Preston nodded, "but that was a story, this one looks thick."

"You'll like it," Guy smirked. "Resistance is futile. You are the oldest I expect you to read it. Then I'll give it to Jordan."

Preston grinned at Guy's 'resistance is futile' line. They had taken to watching *Star Trek: The Next Generation,* reruns after coming in from work

"Where are Walter and Saint?" Preston looked around and frowned.

"They went downstairs." Guy shrugged, "Walter said he had to tour the place to make up his mind about being a doctor or not."

Preston shook his head. Walter's latest obsession was trying to decide whether or not he wanted to be a doctor or a pharmacist. He was searching for his place in life. Just like in the book the Alchemist.

Guy was a quiet genius. Preston had realized this about his brother a long time ago. He was not only book smart. He was people smart. He knew how to handle people. He was quietly manipulating them with his books and his suggestions, and they all followed him.

It shouldn't be possible; Guy was going to be thirteen in a few weeks. Preston wished he had that kind of surety and ease with people.

"Go get them," Preston said. "I'll wake up Case."

Guy slid off his seat and nodded. "So how is Sheryl?"

Preston smiled. "She'll be home by next week."

"That's good news." Guy grinned wide. "Excellent news."

"Yep." Preston nodded.

****

Sheryl looked resentfully out of the car window as Fred drove her mom to the school for parents and teachers day. Fred had to go and represent the boys, and her mom was going to ensure that she had a place for the next school year.

They had removed the bandages from her arm and leg in April. It was too late in the school year for her to go back to school. When her mom sorted it out with the principal, she would more than likely have to redo fourth form, which meant that she would be in the same class as Preston and Jordan. Her life was officially over. She had plans that next school year would be her last. Now, this.

"Life is so unfair," She mumbled. But it was loud enough for her mother to hear. She turned around and gave Sheryl a warning glare.

"Listen to me, Sher. You are not dead. For me, life is very

fair in that regard."

"I might as well be." Sheryl thought in her mind. She didn't want one of her mother's lectures about the being thankful and how blessed she was to be alive. It was not going to do anything for her now. All she could think of was that she was left behind. All of her plans were broken just like her leg, and arm in the accident.

She didn't want to get out of the car when it stopped. She didn't want to go into the school auditorium and meet up her classmates and her teachers.

"You can stay with me while I park," Fred said to her kindly.

Her mother found that acceptable. Sheryl made a face, these days her mother was so overprotective it was nauseating.

"You need to cut her some slack," Fred said finally finding a parking spot at the side of the playfield. "Your mother only wants what's best for you."

"Do you like her?" Sheryl asked Fred.

"Of course I like Miss Pam. She is a good worker and an upstanding woman. I wouldn't have her around the boys if I didn't like her."

"I meant," Sheryl leaned over the front seat and whispered close to Fred's ear, "do you find her attractive?"

"No!" Fred jumped like a scalded cat.

"Do you find me attractive?" Sheryl ran her hand down the side of his cheek.

"Good heavens, no." Fred looked at her in horror. "Sheryl, you feeling okay?"

Sheryl cupped Fred's crotch and then squeezed. "Oh yes. Why wouldn't I be?"

Fred grabbed her hand and twisted it. "Get out of the car."

"Why?" Sheryl asked confused. "I just asked you a simple question."

"I don't know what has gotten into you." Fred hissed, "but I do not find young girls attractive. I am going to tell your mother about this."

Sheryl giggled. "If you tell, I am going to say that you touched me first."

"Here," she cupped her breasts. Why couldn't they have been bigger?

"And then I'll tell her that you stuck your tongue down my throat."

Fred got out of the car a look of fright on his face.

Sheryl found it hilarious. She opened her legs to him and wiggled her tongue. "I know you want me, Freddie."

Fred looked around and then pulled her out of the car. "Stop this now, or I swear I'll break that arm of yours again."

"Threats." Sheryl purred, "does this mean you are going to be rough?"

"For heaven's sake!" Fred stepped away from her and walked away.

"Come and get it, Fred!" Sheryl giggled "It's yours when you want it."

Chapter Seventeen

Sheryl was not the same since the accident. Preston had a sneaky suspicion that something had gone wrong with her personality. She was no longer the reserved, shy girl who loved to read. She was now the adventuress, suggesting that they do stuff that even Shawn was uncomfortable doing.

She was also more touchy-feely and affectionate.

The four of them were supposed to be studying for end of year maths exams. They were sitting at the dining room table, and Sheryl was playing footsie and winking at him from across the table.

He couldn't keep a straight face nor was he sure that he had the willpower to resist her advances. He was contemplating exchanging places with Jordan who was sitting beside her to escape her toes running up and down his pants, but he didn't want Jordan to know what was going on. Sheryl had turned from quiet scholar to seductress. Miss Pam's vigilance was the only thing curtailing their interactions.

If she wasn't around who knows what would go on? Sheryl seemed as if she was up for anything.

Jordan jumped up suddenly and stretched. "Juice break. Anybody want anything?"

Shawn looked at him strangely. "Yes, I'd like some of Miss Pam's Papaya juice that she served at dinner."

"And I'll sit beside Sheryl when you get back."

"Sure." Jordan walked to the fridge and then looked over at him.

"You want anything, Preston?"

"No thanks," Preston said, "only the answer to question 3."

"That's easy," Shawn said. "What's wrong with the two of you, you haven't passed question three?"

"I haven't passed question one." Sheryl grimaced. "It all seems so jumbled to me and what's with all of the exes and the y's."

"It's algebra, duh." Shawn yawned. "And I feel sleepy. It is almost home time."

"Your mother lets you go riding with Jordan in the dark," Sheryl whispered, "Do you guys like stop in the night and touch each other?"

Shawn gasped, and so did he. It was an overtly sexual question. It was not Sheryl-like.

Shawn was about to answer when Miss Pam's footsteps could be heard coming toward the kitchen.

"Sheryl Monica Stone!" Miss Pam entered the kitchen, "are you doing more whispering than working?"

"No," Sheryl said sullenly. "Why do you keep coming in here every ten minutes to check on me?"

"Because I am the study police." Miss Pam retorted. "And I don't trust children to be by themselves for long, especially a bunch of fourteen-year-olds."

"I am fifteen." Preston pointed out. As if anyone could forget. This year had been just as crappy as all of his other birthdays.

The school counselor had suggested that he take some time for himself and just enjoy the day. That had been a luxury that he could not afford, he had work, and he had external exams to sit. He was doing four external examinations this year. That's how he and Jordan had planned it.

To split up their CXC's. Shawn had decided to follow them, in what they had dubbed the get-out-of-school-early plan. Sheryl had barely pulled through her classes the last term, but she had volunteered to study with them.

It was disconcerting to see that she had fallen so far behind. She had been far ahead of the pack but was now barely limping behind and asking outrageous questions that she would not have before. Was this a part of her growing up?

He wondered if he should say something to Miss Pam, but he thought better of it. Miss Pam was already doing a stellar job of keeping her under tabs.

****

"I am telling you, Shawn." Jordan opened his gate. She grabbed my crotch under the table and started to caress me.

"Stop it! Liar!" Shawn was laughing and could hardly keep her bicycle straight. She hopped off and started laughing uncontrollably.

Jackie was still at the salon. The lights were blazing; quite a few cars were parked before the house. Jordan could vaguely remember Jackie saying she had a wedding party of eleven bridesmaids who were doing some elaborate hairstyles.

"So what did she ask you while we were at the table,"

Jordan asked Shawn getting back to the topic at hand, "that caused you to gasp like that, and how did you know that you should switch places with me?"

"You looked uncomfortable." Shawn sobered up. "I had no idea that she was grabbing you under the table. She did ask if we stopped in the dark and touched each other."

Jordan shook his head. "Something is wrong with her… she's a church girl and all. Sweet church girls don't grab people under the table."

Shawn nodded. "That's true. She has been a little strange lately, but it's not as if she is way out there."

"She got D's on a couple of her subjects." Jordan sighed. "It's as if she no longer cares about books and school work and all of that."

"She is just adjusting. She landed on her head in the accident. I am surprised she is even functioning now." Shawn leaned her bicycle on the gate and sat on the veranda step. Jordan sat beside her.

"Preston likes her, you know." Jordan sighed. "I mean he cares about her."

"Yeah." Shawn nodded. "I can see him doing the puppy dog eyes thing with her."

"And she is grabbing me under the table." Jordan whistled. "That's bizarre."

"She did tell me one time that she thought you were both delicious." Shawn giggled, "Maybe she wants to sample both of you."

"Stop the madness," Jordan growled. "I am not sharing any girl with my brother. It's gross."

Shawn took down her curly hair from her ponytail, and a mass of it fell down around her neck and in her back. She caressed her scalp in the half-light.

"I have something to tell you."

"What? You seeing Preston on the sly?"

"No, silly." Shawn looked at him and then groaned. "That's so way off. When would I have time to be sneaking around with your brother?"

"There was a time when you told me you liked him," Jordan said slowly.

"That was a long time ago." Shawn started on her temples again. "I am over that."

"Good," Jordan said in relief, "because you know you are my girl right?"

Shawn stopped caressing her temple and looked at him. It was as if the all the sounds from the night had stopped.

"You can't say stuff like that. We are best friends. You just can't change us. I can't deal with it if we change. There is nobody else in my life like you. I can't allow flimsy little things like romance to come between us."

Jordan sighed. "So you haven't thought about it? You and I...together forever."

"Yes." Shawn stopped rubbing her scalp, "and then I decided that it's too risky. I value our friendship too much."

Jordan frowned. "That's rubbish!"

"People break up all the time." Shawn looked into Jordan's eyes in the half-light. "But friendships last."

"I guess that's true but some people last," Jordan murmured. "My parents lasted, and they were together for a very long time. They have been together since my mom was fourteen."

"Goodness, no." Shawn shook her head. "Your parents were not the best example of a proper relationship. I could not watch you get married to someone else and have a family with them. Nuh uh, no way!

"As for my parents, they are no better. They were friends too, and now my mother is quite fine being the side chick while my dad is married to someone else. That's not for me either. I would not be proud to tell anybody that I am the Jamaican wife like Jackie does. That's madness. I am too special for that!"

"You are." Jordan chuckled because Shawn was getting all worked up. "I would never do that to you."

"You say that now because you are a boy and life hasn't happened yet." Shawn looked at him with disdain, "but you'll turn into a man. And men are not faithful are they. My dad, your dad, hell most of the men I know."

"I will be." Jordan shrugged. "I made that vow years ago, and I will follow it. I will be different from my parents."

Shawn snorted. "You had better be faithful to your girl."

"But it's not going to be you," Jordan said tiredly.

"No, I won't be around." Shawn sighed. "That is kinda what I had to tell you. My father is filing for me to live in the States."

Jordan felt his heart almost stop. He should have expected something like this. He just never expected the words to have such a devastating impact.

Shawn was leaving. It was one of those things that he had grown up fearing. And here it was.

"I am not going until I finish high school," Shawn said morosely. "I will also do SATS next year."

"One whole year to say goodbye," Jordan said dryly. "How fun."

"I told my dad. He wasn't taking no for an answer, worse when I asked him if he could file for you too."

Jordan chuckled. He imagined Shawn telling her father that she wouldn't come to America without Jordan.

"And what did he say?"

"'Sorry Shawn, I have one kid in Jamaica, not two. You are coming to live with me, and that's that.'"

"He is right." Jordan inhaled the night air. The scent in

the air was a mixture of hair products wafting from Jackie's salon and panic, pure unadulterated panic.

He was familiar with the panic—how did you live without your one constant in life. Shawn was his constant. Nobody was as close to him as Shawn was.

He lost his parents years ago, and she was his anchor. And now she was discussing leaving in a calm, collected tone.

"I am not calm," she said as if reading his thoughts. "I've been getting headaches ever since I heard."

Jordan touched her fingers where she was vigorously rubbing her scalp and took over from her. She leaned back into him, and he silently rubbed her head. This was familiar, Shawn's scalp, him rubbing her head for her when she had a headache. It was easier in the past when she didn't have so much hair.

"It's okay," he whispered, "we'll get by. You'll come back often. We'll see each other."

He was trying to be positive.

"Yep." Shawn murmured. "And we'll talk on the phone every single day. I hear that regular people will be able to afford cell phones soon. Jackie is getting one. You can get one. We'll talk every day."

"Yes." Jordan nodded. "We'll talk even more than now."

"That's right." Shawn agreed, a hitch in her voice. "We'll never say goodbye to each other."

"Never, not for us." Jordan sighed. "But it won't be the same."

He withdrew his hands from Shawn's hair and turned her around toward him. "We are already changing. You'll have new sophisticated friends. You'll meet new boys; you won't have the time for me."

"Never," Shawn whispered and swallowed. "It will never happen to us. I will always love you. You will always be my best friend, no matter what."

"Wait right here." Shawn got up and let herself into the house and came back with a pin. She turned on the veranda light.

"What are you doing with that?" Jordan looked from her to the pin.

"Something we should have done a long time ago, reaffirm our commitment in blood." Shawn declared. "Give me your finger."

"Hell no." Jordan tucked his hand under his leg.

"Stop being a wuss." Shawn pricked her finger and a little pearl of blood formed at the tip.

"Now it is your turn, Wiley Girl. It doesn't hurt I promise."

Jordan held out his finger, and she pricked him at the tip and then smeared their blood together.

"Now we are one." Shawn grinned at him pushing her face close to his.

Jordan didn't know what came over him. He mashed his lips to hers clumsily. They were so soft like a mini pillow, and when she gasped under his assault, he deepened the kiss.

He didn't know how long it lasted he was enjoying the sensation too much to care that they were sitting on his veranda under the bright light kissing for all the community to see... Shawn was in it wholeheartedly. So much for her little speech about them just being friends.

She was pulling him closer to her like a drowning man, and he was a lifeboat, and she was making little moaning sounds in her throat or was that him.

There was a squeal of laughter from the salon, and they broke apart reluctantly and looked at each other half dazed.

Their first kiss.

"We have to do this again," Shawn whispered. "Over and over again."

"Shawn," Jordan cleared his throat, "this changes things."

"It changes nothing." Shawn got up and stretched. "We are still best friends. We won't go too far. I think we are over thinking things who better to experiment with than me? And vice versa."

Jordan shook his head. "I don't know..."

"Suck it up, Jordy. We are now officially kiss buddies."

Jordan just shook his head in exasperation. It was easier for girls, this whole intimacy thing. He had to sit on the step and wait for his erection to subside.

****

They got their CXC results in August. Preston got five grade ones—the highest grades in all his subjects. Preston looked at the results in shocked disbelief. He had thought that he would have stumbled with his English.

School was out of session when he got the results, but he already knew that he would be taking just three CXC's in the next school year and then two 'A' level subjects. He was circumventing two years of sixth form, and he was going to do Management Studies at UWI, and then he was going to come and run the family business.

He figured that something was off. The chief accountant had quit at the top of the summer and Fred was squealing that everything was all right in a panic filled voice. It made him feel uneasy. What was more Fred had not replaced Mignot, he and Jordan were practically running the department with Mignot's old assistant.

Fred, the adult, looked quite contented with that.

They had barely scraped through getting payroll right. Talk about a baptism of fire.

"What's your result?" Shawn waved her paper in front of

his face when she stepped out of the office.

"I passed them all," Preston said solemnly. "And you?"

"Me too." Shawn grinned. "I got all ones."

"So did I," Preston smirked.

Shawn looked toward the office door in anticipation of Jordan coming out. And so did Preston.

He wanted his brother to do well, but he was also practical. They had four other brothers to take care of between them. If something were to happen to the business at least both he and Jordan could be employable.

He didn't want to think this way, but Fred was not acting right.

Jordan came through the office with a huge grin.

Preston sighed with relief. What's the result? Three ones. Two, two's. Jordan smirked. I should have left Biology until next year, but it's a pass, and I did have a little difficulty with some of my Physics questions, but the rest of it was ones all the way."

"Those are good grades for science subjects and to think you did two of them at this level." Shawn high-fived Jordan. "Can I just say, I am proud of the two of you Wiley boys." She hooked her hand in theirs. "When we started this high school journey I had no idea that we would be here. Passing our external exams and such."

"Your speech sucks." Jordan gave her a mock growl.

"Want us to go sit under a tree and reminisce," Shawn asked, indicating to an empty graffiti filled bench under a tree which had a view of the beach below.

They sat down together with Shawn in the middle.

"We can't stay long. We have work." Preston hunched his shoulders. "We are the accounts department of Wiley Groceries…two fifteen-year-olds. Can you believe that?"

Shawn shook her head. "It's crazy. Fred is crazy for not

getting anybody. What will happen when you guys start the next school year?"

"Then he'll have Mignot's assistant, Wayne, do all the work."

"Then he too will quit." Shawn sighed. "You both didn't get a chance at a regular childhood did you?"

"What's a regular childhood?" Jordan looked at her cross-eyed.

"Having parents to guide you," Shawn looked from Preston to Jordan, "arguing with them and them telling you what you don't want to hear. Just the guidance."

"Preston has Fred." Jordan shrugged, "and Miss Pam."

"I had Fred and Miss Pam," Preston said contemplatively. "These days I think the adults need more guidance than anything. Both Fred and Miss Pam are acting weird."

"Miss Pam is worried about Sheryl," Jordan said. "To be honest, I am too. I am kind of happy that she is spending the summer with her grandmother in Kingston."

"Me too." Preston nodded. "I think it's for the best. All those rumors about her were getting too much."

"You sure that they were just rumors?" Shawn asked cautiously. "I don't know if you have seen it, but Sheryl has been acting kind of...I don't know... er... sexy."

"Yep." Jordan cleared his throat. "I told him that Sheryl grabbed my crotch under the table and he doesn't believe me. He still refuses to accept that I didn't imagine things."

"I don't want to hear any of that stuff again." Preston stood up and started pacing. "It can't be true. You were mistaken."

"I heard that she was caught in the science lab with the young science teacher. What's his name again? Her hand was in his lab coat, and the teacher was looking guilty," Shawn said, "and this was from a reliable source."

Preston exhaled noisily. "You ready to go? We have loads

of work to do."

"She has not been the same since the accident. Something went wrong." Jordan shook his head. "What if she comes back and tries to touch any of my other brothers. I am going to move them from the house. It's not only girls that can be sexually assaulted."

"That will not happen," Preston said through gritted teeth. "She will be fine when she gets back. She has had a tough year. You all need to cut her some slack and stop listening to rumors." He glared at Shawn.

After he stomped off, he realized that he had left his bag on the bench.

He looked back; Shawn had picked it up for him. She and Jordan were heading toward him at a much slower pace.

He shouldn't be mad at them. They were just misinformed, and in the case of Jordan delusional.

Sheryl was not acting right but to imply that she had turned into a rabid nymphomaniac was just not true.

It can't be. He had feelings for her. Serious feelings.

He didn't feel that way about any other girl. When she got back to Portland after her holiday, he would be watching her closely, and he would be making things official between them.

Chapter Eighteen

September 2001

The new school year started with the kind of business that characterized the start of all school years. It was Preston's final year, and it looked nothing like when he had just begun.

For one, he was not in the same class as Jordan. They were separated into classes that allowed them to focus on their specific academic subjects. Jordan had chosen the sciences and Preston had chosen business. And two, he was no longer an outsider. He didn't have any ridiculous nicknames. One thing remained constant though; he still couldn't wait to get out.

He needed to get started with university and then take over his father's business from Fred before it was too late. The summer's revelations were alarming. Wiley Groceries was hemorrhaging money faster than it was making it and he very much feared that they were in the red.

The accounts said they were in trouble though Fred said they were not. But the numbers don't lie. Preston felt as if a cloud of doom was hanging over his head. Summer walked into the class and sat beside him. She put her hand on her forehead in a swooning gesture.

"Preston Wiley, you are looking especially handsome after the summer. My Gosh, what are you Wiley boys drinking? I just saw Jordan heading to class, and I was like, no way can he get even cuter and taller but he did. And now you... gorgeousnessity personified."

"Gorgeousnessity?" Preston raised a brow and then grinned at Summer. She would always say what was on her mind. She hadn't changed a bit a bit in that regard.

She had gotten prettier too, though he wouldn't admit it to her. She had straightened her hair, and it was long to the point where she was almost sitting on it, and teenaged acne had not marred her honey gold complexion. She was already every teenage boys' fantasy.

Not his though. He had the good sense to know that crushing on Summer was pointless. She tended to rub him the wrong way. She was too inquisitive, too chirpy, too everything. She got annoying fast.

"How was your summer?" Summer pulled her desk closer to his. And settled down for a familiar interview. He had genuinely despaired two years ago when he saw that she was going to be in the same class as him, it was like being under a microscope all the time.

"My summer was full of work," he said it patiently. "I spent most days at the supermarket."

"Is it true that Fred Seaton is gambling out all of the supermarket's money and that the bank will soon repossess you guys?"

Preston's heart nearly stopped. Summer's information was

usually solid. She may be an inquisitive, irritating, know it all but she usually had solid facts.

"Where did you hear that from?" Preston barely squeaked out the question.

"Uh oh," Summer looked at him concerned. "You never knew that Fred was a gambler?"

"No." Preston shook his head, his mind racing.

"So you had no idea that your standard of living was going down?" Summer looked at him like he was an idiot.

"What do you mean?" Preston felt as if his head was swelling.

Summer bit her lip and then rubbed her eyes. "I shouldn't tell you this. I just overheard it okay?"

"Okay." Preston croaked.

"My aunt's boyfriend works at an asset recovery firm in St Ann, and I heard him say that he would be around for the next month because he had business to do here, the Wiley's had defaulted on their debt, and they would be ..."

"We do not have debts," Preston said weakly. "There is no debt on the business or the house or the cars."

Summer looked at him sadly, "Fred is a high stakes gambler, they meet on Woody's boat with other high stakes gamblers, he used the deeds to your house and maybe your business as collateral. He lost big money, and now he has to pay back."

"But they can't take it. It is not his to give." Preston was shaking his head dazedly. "He can't use our business for anything, that's not even legal."

Summer shook her head. "I don't know anything about this sort of thing, but I think maybe you should check it out. I could be wrong."

Preston waited until school was over with keen anticipation. He had to confront Fred about this.

He met Jordan and Shawn at their usual spot near the old gun at the north seawall. He quickly told Jordan what he had learned, and Jordan thought he was joking.

"Maybe Summer was joking," Jordan said weakly when he saw his solemn expression.

Preston felt like how he looked, a nervous, panicked wreck. There were so many things to think about like the fact that their livelihood was at stake, their future was in ruins. They had younger brothers who needed to be taken care of. Walter was in fourth form, Guy was in third form, Saint was in second form, and Case had not started high school yet. They needed funds to run the household. How would six parent-less boys survive?

Miss Pam would have to leave. They couldn't afford to pay her without the supermarket income. "The younger boys would probably go to a boy's home. Life as they knew it would be over."

He didn't realize that he had said the last part out loud.

Jordan was shaking his head. "Life wouldn't be over. We need to get the facts. We need to speak to Fred. Let's go to the supermarket and talk to him."

Fred was not at his desk when they got there. He was on the shop floor dealing with some issue or the other.

Preston and Jordan sat in the office and waited.

Preston was so nervous he couldn't sit still. Fred had not changed the office much. The walls still had the plaques, the framed articles, and the awards from the Chamber of Commerce. He looked at the smiling picture of his mother and father holding him as a baby.

He was sure when they were standing on this ground after the groundbreaking ceremony they had not anticipated that nearly sixteen years later the supermarket would come to this.

"My mother is a murderess who killed my father and a whole slew of other people on my birthday and my cousin is a gambler who squandered my inheritance." Preston slumped his shoulders. "I am from bad stock, Jordan."

Jordan looked at him sympathetically. "You are not them."

"Heard you were waiting for me." Fred walked into the office a sheave of papers in his hand. "Aren't you two supposed to be dressed for work?"

"We want to ask you something," Preston said sitting beside Jordan.

Fred nodded. "If this is about contraceptives and what not, I think I am ready for the talk."

"This is not about contraceptive it's about Wiley Groceries," Preston growled. "Are you a gambler Fred?"

Fred paused for the longest time. Preston felt his temperature skyrocketing.

"I do play a little." Fred shrugged. "Why do you ask?"

"Did you gamble away the house and the business?" Preston held his gaze unwaveringly.

"You are... this is... is..." Fred hung his head.

Preston's heart sank.

"It's not what you think," Fred said hurriedly looking up. "I needed to get into a game, high stakes, they wouldn't accept me otherwise. I told them I was the custodian of Wiley Groceries until you turned eighteen. They accepted me based on that."

Preston melted like a puddle into the back of the chair. He had thought that hearing that his mother had killed his father and Hannah was bad, this was ranking somewhere near up there.

"I kind of," Fred stammered, "I offered the house as payment for my debts. I am squeezing every last bit out of the supermarket to prevent that, but it is not enough. It won't be enough."

"You can't do this," Preston whispered. "You did not sell us out."

"It is already done." Fred had tears in his eyes. "I am sorry Preston and Jordan."

Fred looked at Jordan who had not moved a muscle since his revelations.

"Pack your things and leave," Preston growled. "You are a disgrace."

"Me leaving will not prevent them from taking the house eventually," Fred said wearily. "It's done. It's signed. It's legal. I am your legal guardian. I have the power to use the house, the businesses in any way I saw fit. And I did."

"When were you going to tell us?" Preston asked hoarsely. "When?"

"I thought that it wouldn't be necessary. I have a couple of million dollars left to pay them, and they would give me back the house, you wouldn't have to know, and this would all blow over."

"So you were raping the supermarket and cooking the books?" Jordan asked hoarsely. "That's why Mignot left, and that's why Wayne keeps on saying that the numbers don't lie."

"Yes." Fred sighed. "If you would just be patient, this will be solved. By the time you are ready to take the reigns here the supermarket will be back in the black. You are young you should not be worrying yourselves with business and things. I want you boys to have a good time as teenagers. Do the things of young boys your age. Forget about this."

"You are fired," Preston said grimly.

"You can't fire me until you are eighteen," Fred said with a smug smile on his face, his crocodile tears forgotten. "I checked. Don't worry Preston. This will pass. Forget about it. I know what I am doing. Go be a kid and leave this to me."

****

"My Uncle Tanner, Aunt Sharla's husband, is a lawyer," Jordan said grimly. "As soon as I get home I am going to call him."

They were sitting at the back of the warehouse still in a daze.

"I can't believe he did this." Preston groaned. "I was still hoping this wasn't true."

"He did it." Jordan grimaced. "And then he called us kids and told us to go and play."

"He used to be such a good person," Preston said in disbelief.

"He is an addict." Jordan ran his hands over his face. "A gambling addict in charge of our money. I don't see this ending well. I wouldn't hold out much hope of him paying off his debt either. We are going to need to talk to the other boys. Have a family meeting and sort out living arrangements."

"Not so fast." Preston frowned.

"There is the back room that Dad used as storage. We can clear that out. My mom was going to use it as a nursery. It is big enough for a bedroom. It even has closet space. I am not looking forward to wading through all of the stuff in there. But I guess it's time."

"Jordan..." Preston whispered, "please stop making plans."

Jordan ignored him. "There are five of you and three rooms available. Some of you are going to have to share. I will start clearing out the room today. Then we move furniture from your place to..."

"Stop it!" Preston covered his ear. "Stop it!"

"I've been living alone since I am twelve." It's doable." Jordan got up. "You'll get used to the idea."

Preston looked at Jordan almost cross-eyed. "How are we going to pay for university? Bills? Living expenses?"

"Scholarships." Jordan snapped his fingers. "We have to apply to every single one we can. I thought that maybe next year I could go to Canada do a civil engineer degree. I am going to have to talk to Aunt Sharla about it."

"You'd leave?" Preston widened his eyes. "You can't leave!"

"I would come back, but best of all I would work like a beast to help to pay the bills. Walter and Guy are just a year or two younger than us they can take care of Case and Saint when you go to university."

Preston sighed. He truly felt overwhelmed. He wondered if any fifteen-year-old boy had to suffer through all of these major life decisions.

"Chin up." Jordan touched him on the shoulder. "There are six of us. We can do this. Besides, when I turn sixteen, I will have access to some funds that Dad has in my name. It can help us out."

"And we have property in San San. Fred has no access to these things. We are still not out in the cold. We just need some more years to get things sorted."

Chapter Nineteen

Sheryl was sitting alone in the kitchen just staring into space when Preston got home. The house was eerily silent. None of the other boys were there yet, and Miss Pam was nowhere to be found.

"You didn't come to school today." Preston greeted Sheryl. "I saved a seat for you beside me. Miss Pam said you would be coming later. You never showed."

Sheryl looked at him wearily and then hung her head. "I couldn't..."

"What's wrong?" Preston sat before her and took her hands in his. This was rare physical contact. Miss Pam frowned at this kind of thing, but she just looked so vulnerable. Her mahogany eyes were limpid and lifeless.

"I am not feeling it. I am just not feeling it," Sheryl said desperation lacing her voice. "I want things to go back to how they were."

Preston squeezed her hands and then let it go.

The accident. She was talking about the accident.

"School was so easy. Now it is so hard." Sheryl shook her head and then sighed. "How was your summer?"

"Busy." Preston shrugged. "I worked through it."

"I should have stayed here and done some of that too." Sheryl smiled. It lit up her face and made her appear even prettier.

It hit Preston that he would want to see her smile like this forever. He was just fifteen, but he knew deep emotions when it hit him in the face. Sheryl brought out feelings of empathy he didn't even know he had.

He had the sudden urge to protect her from all the sadness in the world. He wanted her to be happy. He wanted to make her happy.

"How did your summer go?" He asked. "You didn't call. I could have done with a phone call from you."

Sheryl sighed. "I went to summer school. It was okay. The teacher was good, not great, you know."

Preston nodded.

"And my grandmother is obsessed with church. Whenever I wasn't at school, I was at church. Pretty boring. I couldn't even hang with any of my friends without her frowning over my shoulder."

Preston chuckled. "It was kind of like here."

"Yes," Sheryl smiled. "Mama is gone for the pastor now. She is convinced I have demons."

Preston blanched. "Why?"

"Because I need to be touched." Sheryl turned her eyes to him and winked. "I need it, Preston. I feel as if I will go crazy without it. She caught me touching myself, and when I told her that I had to do it, she raced out of here to go get the pastor to drive them out."

Preston frowned. "Sheryl..."

"And the headaches," Sheryl went from femme fatale to ailing innocent, "I can't stand the headaches. I get them pretty regularly these days. They are sharp they don't last long, but I feel one coming on now."

She leaned back in the chair and closed her eyes, a grimace on her face.

Preston sat there looking at the column of her throat. Her hair was in two fat ponytails that flirted with the top of her breasts.

He dragged his eyes away. *Could she be demon possessed for real? Should he be looking at a demon-possessed girl like that?*

But this was no ordinary demon-possessed girl; this was Sheryl. His Sheryl. His heart ached when he saw how she was suffering.

"Sheryl," he whispered when she was sitting so long with her head bent over that he started fearing for her neck. "I read that touching yourself is a normal part of growing up. Counselor Johns said it was a normal part of a developing sexuality."

Sheryl slowly lifted her head and then looked at him with earnest brown eyes.

"Preston, I do need help. I have done stuff I can't even tell you. Maybe Mama is right. Maybe I need spiritual intervention. I am not me anymore."

Preston felt strange. "What do you mean you've done stuff. You mean the rumors about you are true?"

"It depends on which one." Sheryl shrugged. "This summer I had sex with my summer school teacher, the next door neighbor, and a taxi guy, don't know his name. He gave me money after."

Preston swallowed convulsively. He didn't hear right. Today he was ricocheting between one bad news after the other.

"I don't care who it is," Sheryl said, "I don't even think it is wrong. My grandmother caught me with the next-door neighbor, and I didn't care. I know I shouldn't I was never like this before."

"My God." Preston shook his head. "Sheryl this is..."

"I know, I am a slut." Sheryl laughed, "want us to go upstairs and do it. I won't tell anyone."

"No!" Preston squeaked out the denial. He would say yes but what would that make him? Sheryl was obviously not right.

"What's with the men in this house?" Sheryl sneered. "I did ask Fred, and he said no like a wuss. He has been avoiding me since and now you. Maybe I should ask Walter; he seems like he could be up for it or Guy, he is turning into a hottie. It is possible that he could be the hottest brother. You know what, I don't care which one of you it is. I just need a man."

Preston watched in shock as she got up from the chair and started to remove her clothes. She was down to her panties before he had the presence of mind to react. After all, he just saw breasts live for the very first time. They were small but perfect.

He needed to stop drooling and move. He needed to find the willpower to resist. But the insidious thought crept up in his head, *if she was having sex with the whole neighborhood why not me?*

She was breathing heavy and on the verge of wiggling out of her panties when a startled scream jolted Preston from his mesmerized frozenness.

"Sheryl!" Miss Pam was at the door with Pastor Tate and Miss Adalynn slightly behind her.

Sheryl looked up at them languidly. "Yes, mother."

"Put on your clothes this minute!" Miss Pam was almost

incoherent with anger. "Now, this minute!"

"Told you she was a sourpuss." Sheryl winked at Preston but then turned to the pastor her slim body gloriously naked, her panties around her ankles. "I think you should exorcise these demons out of me naked, pastor. It would work better that way."

"Sheryl!" Miss Pam grabbed her arm and frog-marched her through the kitchen and toward the back door.

"Mama you are hurting me!" Sheryl wailed, "Let me go, I want to have sex with Preston!"

Preston looked at the pastor and his wife red-faced.

"It looks like we came just in time," Pastor Tate gave him a stern look. "Has she ever done this before?"

"Not with me." Preston croaked. "She was just telling me that she just needed a man. Apparently, any male will do."

"That girl is not suffering from demon possession," Miss Adalynn said. "She has a brain injury. Brain trauma can cause compulsive sexual desires. I told you about a similar case in Montego Bay, where the girl met in an accident she damaged her frontal lobe, this part of the head." Miss Adalynn pointed to her forehead.

"Apparently if this part of the brain is damaged it can mess with self-control, foresight, attention, and reasoning.

"I think what Sheryl is suffering from is hypersexuality disorder. It can be treated. She needs a brain scan to determine the extent of the damage to her frontal lobe and to work out a treatment plan."

Pastor Tate cleared his throat. "Well then, we can still pray with Miss Pam and then you can help her to find a professional who specializes in this issue."

Miss Pam came back into the kitchen looking disheveled and embarrassed. "I am so sorry, Pastor. I don't know how demons came into our house. I monitor what they read. I monitor the television shows. I make sure that they pray every day. I see to it that we have worship. Of course, it's harder over here with five boys. Who knows what they get up to in the privacy of their rooms?

"But I watch my daughter like a hawk. The Lord delivered her from the accident, and there is no way I am going to leave her up to the devil!"

"Sis. Pam," Miss Adalynn said gently, "maybe you should take a seat and hear what I think. Some things are not so simplistically explained away. Some things like in Sheryl's case may have a scientific reason."

Miss Pam sat down reluctantly. She heard everything that Miss Adalynn said and nodded politely. She participated in the prayers and then she saw the pastor and his wife out.

"They are too modern for my taste," she said after she closed the front door behind them. "I know a demon possession when I see it."

"But Miss Pam," Preston said, "at least give them a listening ear."

"No!" Miss Pam glared at him. "My baby is not brain damaged. She is still recovering from a horrible accident and is demon possessed. Maybe she got it at the hospital. I am not about to put her through any more tests! Next time, I will get my own church pastor instead of these sciency professionals!"

Chapter Twenty

His sixteenth birthday, the day was shaping up to be a bright one. It was the kind of Sunday that you thought twice about getting out of bed. It was overcast and had rained that morning.

Miss Pam had her church clothes on and was humming as she flitted around the kitchen.

"Happy birthday, Preston Wiley!"

She gave him a broad smile. Her voice echoed through the house.

The house was like a mausoleum. Fred had pawned off most of the furniture. The ones he deemed as unnecessary.

He claimed it was to help to get rid of his debt. It could be to sell so that he could gamble it away. Preston wasn't sure which and he was at his wit's end with Fred.

They were only in April, and it felt as if the year had run its course already. He was seriously thinking of moving to Jordan's place. Walter and Guy were all but living there.

They had practically moved out over the Christmas.

They preferred to be living in a place that wasn't so depressing and nearly empty.

Preston couldn't blame them.

Everybody was waiting for the shoe to drop. Uncle Tanner had flown out in January to assess the real state of affairs and was not pleased. He had grimly told the boys that they should expect the worse. There was nothing that he could do except to sue for guardianship of the boys, a feat that was almost impossible with him living in Canada. Besides, he had his own growing family to look after.

Fred's mother Glenda had offered to be their guardian, but she had gotten a call to consult in Saudi Arabia and had called from the airport with her apologies.

They were stuck with Fred. And he knew it.

Irresponsible gambler, Fred. They would have had a better time of it with a cat as their guardian.

"When are your brothers coming over?" Miss Pam asked, "the ones that don't live here anymore?"

She sniffed. She was still hurt that Walter and Guy had left.

"Maybe later," Preston said.

"Is Jordan coming too?" Miss Pam asked sweetly. "These days he is too busy to visit."

"I would think so." Preston nodded. "He always comes over for my birthday."

"Well then. I will cook a fine meal," Miss Pam said chirpily, "and I will bake a cake as soon as I get back from church."

"You don't have to, Miss Pam," Preston said quickly.

"It is not a problem, Preston. I am quite willing to do it. I still get paid to take care of you boys."

"Can Sheryl eat with us?" Preston asked eagerly. He was longing to see her. She never came over to the house anymore. Miss Pam had practically imprisoned her in the pool house.

He hardly saw her at school either. She was in fourth form. Poor Sheryl. She spent nearly three years in fourth form and was still struggling.

"Of course she can join you," Miss Pam said. "She is doing well these days almost demon free. She is even eating more and has fewer headaches. God is good. When we get back from church, she will help with the meal."

Preston had to admit that maybe Miss Pam's assessment had not been way off about Sheryl being demon possessed. She had gotten a bush doctor, Dr. Sam Fay, to come by the house three times per week to perform all sorts of rituals on Sheryl and give her herbal concoctions. It seemed to be doing the trick—she wasn't losing it like before.

Miss Pam was significantly happier because of it.

"So what are you doing for your birthday?" Miss Pam asked. "I might practice driving. I have my learner's license, but I am not going on the road. I will practice behind the house. I can even teach Case and Saint."

"Good." Miss Pam turned away, still humming.

And he did have a good time with his brothers for the day. They took out his mother's BMW and took turns driving and doing stunts with it on the back lawn.

It was the best birthday he had ever had.

Until they were seated around the dining room table.

Even Fred was home early presumably to celebrate with him.

"I will officially teach you to drive, Preston. I saw you having fun outside."

Preston was feeling resentful toward Fred. He wanted to say no, but he needed an experienced driver to take him on the road.

"And you too Jordan," Fred smiled congenially. "That will be my birthday present to both of you this year."

"Thanks," Preston said grudgingly.

"I can't wait," Jordan nodded. "Dad's jeep is sitting at the house unused just waiting for me to get my hands on."

"And mine," Walter said. "It will be my pleasure to learn how to drive."

They started talking about cars, a subject that was bound to cause excitement and vigorous discussions.

Fred was in the middle of describing his first trip to Dover raceway and his first taste of handling a powerful car to their rapt attention when they heard a crash in the kitchen.

And then a horrified, "What!" from Miss Pam.

They looked at each other in alarm. Fred was pushing his chair away from the table to investigate when Miss Pam walked into the dining room with a carving knife in one hand with the other pulling Sheryl by her dress.

She was fuming.

She loosened her fingers from the back of Sheryl's periwinkle blue dress and then tangled it in hair. Holding her head at an awkward angle.

Preston winced on Sheryl's behalf. He was about to protest her rough treatment when Miss Pam started waving the carving knife around.

"Which one of you sickos impregnated my daughter?"

A collective gasp was uttered around the table. The boys looked at each other.

Preston felt his heart sink. Was Sheryl pregnant?

His eyes traveled down from the knife Miss Pam was waving about to Sheryl's belly. It still looked flat to him.

"Now listen Miss Pam," Fred held up his hand, "put down the knife!"

"Oh no," Miss Pam shook her head furiously, "whoever

impregnated Sheryl is going to have to marry her, and I am not joking. You think that you can take my daughter's innocence and then leave her pregnant. Oh no, this is not happening under my watch."

"What makes you think that any of the boys did it?" Fred frowned, "and unless you have been living under a rock, Sheryl is not innocent. She has propositioned me once. I have made sure that she is never alone in my presence."

"Liar!" Miss Pam squealed. "My Sheryl would never do that. I didn't know you were a pervert, Fred."

"Me?" Fred blanched. "Hold on a second, Miss Pam, you seem to have a blind spot where your daughter is concerned."

"No, I don't," Miss Pam growled. She tugged Sheryl closer to the table.

"Sheryl, who got you pregnant? You said it was one of the Wiley boys which one?"

Sheryl started to sob.

"Mama, please!"

"No crying, no pleading, nothing will get you off the hook." Miss Pam turned to look at them. "I don't care who it is, even if it is eight-year-old Case, you are going to marry my daughter. I will not be shamed."

Sheryl looked like a frightened animal caught in headlights. Preston's heart went out to her. There was always a soft spot for Sheryl in his heart.

"It's either Preston or Jordan," Sheryl whispered in the silence. "I am not sure which one."

"What do you mean you are not sure?" Miss Pam choked out the question. "You had sex with both boys?"

"Yes." Sheryl nodded. "Both of them. Almost the same day."

Preston straightened up in the chair in alarm. *Had Jordan had sex with Sheryl?*

Jordan was not taking any of it seriously. He laughed and hit the table, but he sobered up quickly when he saw that all eyes were on him.

"That's a lie from the pit of hell!"

Miss Pam turned her eyes on Preston almost hopefully. She could see the righteous indignation in Jordan's face; she knew he was not joking around.

It was down to him. All her hopes rested on him being the father. At least with him, she could save face. Her daughter would not look like some sex-starved nymphomaniac who was brain damaged.

It was tragic to see the desperation on her face.

And then he looked at Sheryl.

She desperately wanted him to save her from her mess. He wondered if he loved her enough to do it, to own a child at this point in his life when he didn't even know how he would manage himself and his brothers.

He was just sixteen years old, and though he liked her and had a soft spot for her, he was too young to take this on.

She was too young for this. It would not be right for her either. Her situation was tragic enough, what she needed was real help, not a forced marriage.

Jordan kicked him under the table. He had not realized how long he had been silent and had them in suspense. Everybody was looking at him with a question in their eyes.

Was he Sheryl's baby daddy?

"No," he said it out loud, "it's not me. Sorry, Sheryl."

His brothers breathed a sigh of relief. Even Fred looked relieved. Miss Pam lowered the knife—tears in her eyes.

"I er we are going to have to move back to Kingston after the school year, six more weeks." She cleared her throat. "We can't stay here."

Fred nodded. "That's understandable."

"Who is the father?" Walter asked curiously. He had been quiet until now.

Miss Pam loosened her hand from Sheryl's hair and turned to look at her daughter.

"Dr. Sam Fay," Sheryl whispered, "the bush doctor. He said it was part of the therapy."

"Good Lord!" Miss Pam crossed her heart. "I am going to kill him. He took advantage of a sick girl...I am going to kill him, lord..."

She marched toward the kitchen.

Everybody got up and went after her.

"Miss Pam," Fred said calmly. "I think what we need to do is to talk to the police about this. Sheryl is still only fifteen. This is a criminal act."

Miss Pam slumped on the kitchen island and started to howl. Sheryl joined her mother in the sobbing.

Jordan looked at Preston and shook his head. "I am going home, too much drama here."

"I'll come with you," Preston offered. "Let me go for my school stuff for tomorrow."

It didn't escape him that it was one more year when he had no appetite for his birthday cake and that his world always collapsed on his birthday.

Chapter Twenty-One

They lost the house in June. The very last day of school. It was sold to a property developer who wanted to turn it into a hotel. They lost the supermarkets in July. Fred had run them to the ground and borrowed from the banks using them as collateral.

Wiley Groceries was closed indefinitely.

Miss Pam moved back to Kingston with Sheryl and Fred was nowhere to be found. There were rumors that he sailed away with Woody in the middle of the night. He didn't even leave a note.

The Wiley brothers were on their own.

They were all living at their father's house. They had settled into some semblance of normality. With no adult to supervise they had quickly worked out a system of governance which made the household run smoother.

Preston had gotten high grades in his external exams and a scholarship to the College of Arts, Science and Education, his father's alma mater. Jordan had also passed his subjects, but he would continue at the high school for sixth form. He needed some A levels for his Canadian university of choice. He would be around for his brothers, especially Case when he entered high school.

In August Jordan had gone with Jackie to the airport to see off Shawn to the States. He had been privately crying in his room ever since. It was as if all the stuffing had been knocked out of him.

They could tell that he was suffering, but he didn't want to talk about it.

It was up to Preston to flex his big brother muscles and keep the troops together.

He was up for the task. This summer had come with the kind of clarity that he had not known he possessed.

It was as if he had grown up overnight as if something had clicked in his head and he could clearly see the path he should go.

His number one priority was caring for his brothers, ensuring that they stayed together and out of trouble.

He didn't have the energy for anything else.

He didn't want to think about Miss Pam leaving with Sheryl. He didn't want to think about what he had done.

He was sitting on the back veranda staring at Guy's vegetable patch when Jordan sat beside him.

"She's gone." Jordan sighed. "This is the suckiest summer ever. A summer without Shawn is no summer at all."

"I wondered when you would talk about it." Preston glanced at him, "you better now?"

"No, I still feel as if someone cut off a limb." Jordan shrugged. "But life goes on. People live without their limbs all the time."

"Yep." Preston nodded. "That they do."

"So aren't you going to tell me?" Jordan looked at him with knowing eyes.

"Tell you what?" Preston looked at him and then away guiltily.

Jordan sighed. "That you slept with Sheryl. I know you did. I could see the fear on your face when Miss Pam dragged her to the table on your birthday. I also know she didn't want to get you in trouble that is why she called my name as a potential father for her child."

Preston swallowed and shook his head. "This is crazy you know?"

"Yep." Jordan nodded. "What the hell happened? What about the speech about being responsible and not being like Dad?"

"She came into my room naked, slid into the bed with me and started touching me. What was I to do?"

"Flee. Run. Hide." Jordan shook his head. "Do something other than have sex with her."

"It felt too good," Preston whispered. "I was too far gone when I realized what was happening. I didn't care that Miss Pam would find us. I didn't care that she was sick in the head and probably acting off some strange impulse or that she would sleep with anybody once they moved. I didn't care about anything. I lost my senses for a while."

Jordan groaned. "I get it, I do, but the consequences bro, the consequences. That baby could be yours you know that, right? Yours could be the lucky sperm that fertilized her egg."

Preston nodded. "I know that but then again it might not be, and I wasn't going to throw away my future because of a maybe. I am just sixteen years old! I have lost everything, my parents, the businesses, the house, how was I to take on a wife that is mentally unstable and a baby that may not be mine."

Jordan sighed. "Miss Pam was threatening with that knife. For a moment there I thought you would...."

"Maybe I should have," Preston said doubtfully. "It would be the right thing to do. I think I love Sheryl. I think we could make it work."

"How would it work?" Jordan glared at him. "I didn't bring this up for you to get all regretful and stuff. I brought it up because I wanted you to know that you don't have to carry this around on your own. I am here to support you if you want to talk about it."

Preston nodded. "Thanks."

"We still have some growing up to do and a couple of brothers to see through the worse. We have to work together to see that happen."

"Yes, " Preston sighed. "What do you think the future will hold for us?"

"Long term… I think we will all make it through, be successful in life. Short term we are in for a rough ride, but we'll do it together."

"Together." Preston echoed. "The Wiley brothers will survive and thrive together."

The End

Author's Notes

Dear Reader,

This is the beginning of a new and exciting series. I can't wait to delve into the story of each Wiley brother. Preston's story is next; an excerpt from that book- **For Pete's Sake** is on the next page.

Don't worry; you will see Jordan and Shawn again in **Crossing Jordan**. Walter, Guy, Saint, and Case will all get their stories in upcoming books.

As usual, thank you for reading my work.

Thanks again. All the best,

Brenda

Here is an excerpt from For Pete's Sake
(Wiley Brothers Book 1)

"Mr. Preston Wiley, thank you so much for this interview. Your secretary said that she wasn't sure that you had the time." Denise gazed at her handsome interviewee and tried not to drool.

Preston nodded and looked at his watch. "I am pressed for time today. Is ten minutes okay? What was your name again?"

"Denise Graham, from Caribbean Finance Magazine. I am not sure that ten minutes will do, sir. Your life is a fascinating one. We covered you before in our Millionaires Under Twenty-five issue, and we got hints of a great story. We thought that this time around we would feature you on the cover and run your life story."

"My life story?" Preston furrowed his brow and then chuckled. "I am not too keen on my life story being in the public sphere, Denise."

A knock on the door interrupted their conversation, and a striking looking man walked into the office.

"Sorry to interrupt." His voice sounded less than apologetic, but Denise was not paying that any mind. She was too awestruck even to process the thought. He had a faint resemblance to Preston Wiley, so she concluded that he was one of the Wiley brothers, he had to be. This one was certifiably hot.

"Can I have a quick word with you Preston?"

"Hello there." He smiled at her warmly

How do the females in this building get any work done? Denise thought dazedly.

"This is Denise from Caribbean Finance Magazine," Preston said to his brother, "and Denise this is Walter Wiley, vice president of Finance."

"Nice to meet you." Denise nodded at Walter. "Is it possible for me to get a mini-interview with you too Walter?"

"Oh, not today." Walter glanced at his watch. "Call my assistant and set it up though. I think I can accommodate you later this week."

"Thank you." Denise nodded.

Preston got up and they headed to the far corner of the office where they stood shoulder-to-shoulder and whispered about God knows what.

Denise wished she could hear, but she would settle for observing them. What an eyeful it was.

She was a professional journalist who had been covering people in business for well nigh two decades, but it did not take a genius to figure out that the Wiley brothers were a fascinating bunch.

Goodness, if everything she had heard about Preston Wiley and his brothers was true, she had an epic article on her hands.

So far the accounts of how handsome they were held true. Maybe everything else was as well. She had a whole bunch of notes from reliable sources about their fascinating lives.

There were stories about how they grew up without parents. How one set of them, she wasn't sure which set, had a mother who killed the other mother because she got tired of sharing her husband, Joseph Wiley.

If their father looked anything like them, I can understand why women were willing to share him and kill for him, Denise thought morbidly.

The brothers had hooded eyes, short straight noses, pronounced cheekbones and full lips and they were both tall, maybe over six feet.

Standing beside each other now the differences between

the two brothers were obvious. Preston was leanly muscular. He looked more like he had a swimmers body. His hair was clipped close to his head, and he was cleanly shaven.

Walter, on the other hand, was muscular and thick. She could see through his dress shirt that he had some serious biceps especially standing as he was now with his arms folded. He had a neat mustache and beard combo going on that made him look even more attractive.

When two sets of brown eyes suddenly turned her way she resisted the urge to pretend that she hadn't been observing them intently.

They had caught her looking. The only thing she could do was withstand the stares, not breaking eye contact until Walter told them goodbye and strode away from the office.

"Walter just brought a matter to my attention…can we walk and talk? I have to go deal with this situation," Preston said when he came back over to the desk.

"Sure." Denise jumped up, "It would be nice to see you in action."

Preston frowned. "Unfortunately, you won't be seeing me in action. What I am about to do, does not require my area of expertise as the company president; I rarely handle situations like this."

"What is it?" Denise was intrigued.

Preston opened the office door for her. "After you."

"Thank you." Denise smiled.

"A young man just attempted to steal some goods. He is at the Security Center. I hope you wore comfortable shoes," Preston said as they headed down the hallway and towards the elevator of the central administration building.

"I did." Denise looked down at her red pumps. She had come prepared for a tour of the head office of Wiley Corp.

It was a relatively large complex. A Wiley Groceries

supermarket, the core business, was at the heart of the place and the various other companies which were Wiley run, were arranged in a neat U fanning out beside the supermarket. They also had a huge parking lot that was almost always full, even in the nights. She knew because she was a regular shopper.

There was the farming supplies store that was run by Guy Wiley, an architect's firm that was run by Jordan Wiley and a recording studio where Case Wiley, the famous gospel singer, and producer, spent most of his time.

This was indeed the Wiley brothers' headquarters. Her editor had requested a feature with all the brothers. Denise was almost salivating at the thought. It was hard to get them all in one place, so she was fortunate to get Preston Wiley, the head of the company.

She had also interviewed Jordan Wiley, a few years ago for the millionaires under twenty-five and she had wanted both him and Preston to do a joint feature, but it was not meant to be. Jordan was in Dubai finishing up a building project.

Architecture was his passion. She remembered how excited he was about the subject when she spoke to him over the phone.

She dragged her mind from Jordan Wiley and focused on the current Wiley.

What was so special about a young man that stole goods? This was Kingston, even though they had state of the art security, they must catch shoplifters on a regular basis and dealt with them accordingly.

"Can we get on with the interview?" Preston asked when they got on the elevator. "As I said, today is not exactly ideal in terms of time."

"Oh yes, sorry." Denise whipped out her recorder and turned it on.

"Mr. Wiley, can you tell me about your beginnings, where were you born, that sort of thing?"

"Call me Preston." He looked at the recorder and then at her and shook his head, "Necessary evil, huh?"

She nodded. "I transcribe my notes from it.."

"Okay," Preston shrugged, "I was born in Portland, Jamaica. Have you been there?"

"Me?" Denise smiled, "just once…a wedding at a gorgeous hotel there. I thought how unspoiled it seemed…a place with potential."

"It's a very nice place," Preston said, "very rustic. I try to go back every month or so."

"And your parents," Denise asked, "are they still alive?"

They exited the elevator, and Preston glanced at her.

"It is common knowledge that my mother killed my father, his mistress and his mistress' sister and then herself, leaving six boys and three baby girls behind. She did it on my thirteenth birthday. Needless to say, my birthdays tend not to be very happy ones. That kind of event has a tendency to follow you around."

"Wow! So how did all of you manage?"

"Ah well, the Pryce girls were taken by their brother and his wife. And the six boys were left in the care of my mother's cousin, Fred and the housekeeper Pamela Stone. Fred was appointed our official guardian. At the time, he was heading up the supermarket business and living at the house. I guess it was the practical solution to not have us move and to keep the boys together. My brother Jordan was having none of it though. He would not leave our father's house."

"How old was he?" Denise asked.

"Twelve." Preston smiled. "He lived alone from the age of twelve."

"And what about the rest of you?" Denise asked as they

headed across the lobby to the main entrance of the building.

"We were good for a while," Preston said wryly, "but then we found out that Fred was a gambler and he was not very careful with our inheritance. He wrecked the business by the time Jordan and I turned sixteen. We lost everything, the house, the businesses..."

"Oh, wow!" Denise looked at the large complex. "So how did you come from zero to this in twelve years?"

"It wasn't easy," Preston said. They headed toward the building that said Wiley Security Services.

"Fortunately for us, our father had the foresight to have an investment at the bank that was quite substantial. He saved all thirteen years of profit distribution from running Wiley Groceries. It matured that summer when we thought we had nothing left."

"Amazing, what a coincidence." Denise breathed.

"I don't believe in coincidences." Preston smiled. "I firmly believe that God knows the beginning from the end and he makes provisions for unforeseen circumstances."

"Amen," Denise murmured. "So what did you do with your windfall?"

"The four oldest boys went to college. I went to the local college on a scholarship, Jordan went to the University of the West Indies open campus in Portland. We both did business studies.

"As soon as we hit eighteen we bought back the businesses from the bank and worked like crazy to get them back in black. Those early years were crazy-no-sleep years. We had one goal, and that was to become profitable again while we juggled school.

"All the brothers had to work. It was not an option. Unfortunately, we didn't have the luxury of being typical teenagers. There was no time for anything else in our life."

"Oh, come on." Denise looked impressed. "You never had a girlfriend?"

"I had no time for relationships," Preston said shaking his head. "Between helping our youngest brothers, running a household and two supermarkets I only started looking around when I was twenty-two. I had a semi-serious relationship when I was twenty-three."

"Have you forgotten how to have fun?" Denise asked smiling, "all work and no play..."

"These days I play," Preston said glancing at Denise. "I understand the need for play and also for balance. Now that we have a Wiley Groceries in every parish in Jamaica and we have competent managers and staff. I can breathe a little."

"And how do you relax?" Denise asked they were standing in the middle of the foyer of Wiley Securities.

"I go to Portland. I have a villa there. I snorkel, fish, play tennis and read. My brother Guy is always recommending books to me."

"It sounds tame for a young man of twenty-seven." Denise raised an eyebrow skeptically.

"It is the pace I like." Preston grinned. "Slow, is a welcome pace compared to the catastrophe of my growing up years."

"Any of the Wiley brothers married yet?" Denise asked eagerly, too eagerly.

"No." Preston chuckled at her expression, "but my brother Saint is engaged. He will get married in May."

"And you? When are you planning to tie the knot?" Denise asked.

"I don't know," Preston answered the questioned contemplatively. "I have never really thought about it. I like to think I have plenty of time."

"Have you broken any hearts?" Denise asked.

"This is on the record?" Preston eyed the recorder and then

laughed. "I am not sure if I have. None of my relationships have been long term. As I said, I have been obscenely busy through the years."

"Any regrets in your life so far?" Denise asked smiling.

She was surprised that Preston took a long time to respond. So long in fact that she thought he wasn't going to bother answering.

When he did, he did so with surprising honesty. "Yes, I have one regret. I wouldn't call it a regret more like a mistake I made. Sometimes, I find myself dwelling on it, and I wonder about it especially now that I have more downtime."

"Is it business or personal?" Denise asked.

"Personal, very personal," Preston said, and then he looked across the lobby as a tall, fit gentleman in gym gear strode towards them.

He had the high forehead and the hooded eyes of the Wiley's, but surely he couldn't be a Wiley. He had green eyes, and he was light skinned.

Denise stared in fascination as he came towards them.

"I have him in the holding room," The guy said to Preston. "Let me know how it goes. Call me. I am late for an appointment."

He strode away with Denise looking after him in puzzlement.

"Who is he?"

"That is my brother, Saint. He heads Wiley Security."

"Oh my goodness, he is fine." Denise breathed.

Preston laughed out loud, "That is the reaction that Saint usually gets when he steps into a room. He and Case are the designated heartthrobs of the Wiley brothers."

"You would all get that reaction. I can't imagine the six of you together in the same room. The ladies wouldn't know where to look."

Preston laughed. "Thank you for the compliment, Denise, but I am afraid that this is where I have to leave you. I have to deal with this shoplifting situation privately."

"What is so special about this person?" Denise asked curiously.

"Turn off the recorder first," Preston said waiting for her to turn it off.

She did quickly.

"Well this young man, claims to be the grandson of our former housekeeper Pamela Stone, the one who took care of us after our parents died. I am just going to verify. If he is her grandson, then you must understand that this is a special situation."

"Yes, yes, maybe that could be something for another article?" Denise nodded vigorously. "As it is now, I have more than enough information for my current article. Thank you for your time, Preston. "

Preston nodded. "I hope it will be a good one, and that Wiley Incorporated will be highlighted favorably."

"Yes, definitely." Denise nodded.

She watched in admiration as he headed toward the holding area. His mind was already a million miles away from the magazine article.

OTHER BOOKS BY BRENDA BARRETT

Wiley Brothers Series

Between Brothers (Book 0)- The beginning of the Wiley brothers saga, Joseph Wiley's unconventional family life may prove to be fatal to some members of the family.

For Pete's Sake (Book 1)- Preston has a run in with a child named Pete who claims that he is the grandson of their former housekeeper Pamela Stone.

Crossing Jordan (Book 2)- Jordan is miffed when Shawn takes her new fiancé to Jamaica and insists that he be best man at their wedding.

Fire and Walter (Book 3)- Walter's shady past is affecting his new appointment as church elder. The situation would not only compromise him but a particular newly married church sister as well.

The Perfect Guy (Book 4) - Guy decides to explore the world of farming, becomes an apprentice to a farmer and lives a humble life. He is constantly rebuffed by the woman that he loves because she thinks he is poor!

The Patience of A Saint (Book 5)- Saint attends his own divorce party put on by his soon to be ex wife and they end up complicating matters.

A Case of Love (Book 6)- Case unwittingly buys a bride

from a human trafficking ring a few days before his own wedding.

Resetter Series

Never Too Late (Book 1)- Addi finds out she is a resetter and goes back to the summer of 92 to change her family's lives.

Never Say Never (Book 2)- Skyler's handsome college lecturer, who happens to be her neighbor, has a 't' in his palms. Should she tell him the significance of it. If she does, would he believe her?

Now or Never (Book 3)- Ten years later Addi and Randy meet again at Randy's engagement party. Why is it that the chemistry between them was still so potent? Can they ever have a future together? Would Randy choose her this time around?

Almost Never (Book 4)- Tech genius Joshua Porter had all but given up on love. He then meets Portia, an inmate at the female penitentiary and his life takes a turn for the adventurous.

The Scarlett Family Series

Scarlett Baby (Book 1)- When the head of the Scarlett family died, Yuri had to return home to Treasure Beach for the funeral. What he didn't count on was seeing Marla, his childhood sweetheart and his best friend's wife. And when emotions overwhelm them and a few months later Marla is pregnant, Yuri wants the impossible: his best friend's wife and the baby they made together...

Scarlett Sinner (Book 2)- Pastor Troy Scarlett realizes the hard way that some sins are bound to be revealed, like the child that he had out of wedlock with his wife's mortal enemy from college. His wife Chelsea was not happy with the status quo. She was not taking care of the son of the woman she had so despised from college. And she could not get over the deep betrayal that she felt from her husband's indiscretion.

Scarlett Secret (Book 3)- Terri Scarlett had a soft spot for her friend, Lola. She was funny and sweet and they looked remarkably alike. But when Lola's Arab prince demands his bride, Terri foolishly exchange places with her friend and they meet up on a world of trouble.

Scarlett Love (Book 4)- Slater always looked forward to delivering packages to the law firm where he could get a glimpse of the stunning female lawyer, Amoy Gardener. Unfortunately, for Slater a woman like Amoy would not take him seriously, especially when she found out that he could not read!

Scarlett Promise (Book 5)- Driven by desperation Lisa Barclay decides to make some extra money by prostituting herself after being kicked out in the streets. Her first customer turns out to be a popular government senator and then to her horror he dies...

Scarlett Bride (Book 6)- When Oliver Scarlett's missionary work in the Congo region was coming to an end, he had a decision to make, marry Ashaki Azanga and save her from being the fourth wife to the chief of the village or leave her to her fate and get on with his life...

Scarlett Heart (Book 7)- After receiving a heart transplant shy librarian Noah Scarlett started to take on character traits that were unlike him and he kept dreaming of a girl named Cassandra Green...

Rebound Series

On The Rebound- For Better or Worse, Brandon vowed to stay with Ashley, but when worse got too much he moved out and met Nadine. For the first time in years he felt happy, but then Ashley remembered her wedding vows...

On The Rebound 2- Ashley reinvented herself and was now a first lady in a country church in Primrose Hill, but her obsessed ex friend Regina showed up and started digging into the lives of the saints at church. Somebody didn't like Regina's digging. Someone had secrets that were shocking enough to kill for...

Magnolia Sisters

Dear Mystery Guy (Book 1)- Della Gold details her life in a journal dedicated to a mystery guy. But when fascination turns into obsession she finds herself wanting to learn even more about him but in her pursuit of the mystery guy she begins to learn more about herself...

Bad Girl Blues (Book 2)- Brigid Manderson wanted to go to med school but for the time being she was an escort working for her mother, an ex-prostitute. When her latest customer offers her the opportunity of a lifetime would she take it? Or would she choose the harder path and uncertain love with a Christian guy?

Her Mistaken Dreams (Book 3)- Caitlin Denvers dream guy had serious issues. He has a dead wife in his past and he was the main suspect in her murder. Did he really do it? Or did Caitlin for the first time have a mistaken dream?

Just Like Yesterday (Book 4)- Hazel Brown lost six months of memory including the summer that she conceived her son, and had no idea who his father could be. Now that she had the means to fight to get him back from the Deckers, she finds out that the handsome Curtis Decker is willing to share her son with her after all.

New Song Series

Going Solo (Book 1)- Carson Bell, had a lovely voice, a heart of gold, and was no slouch in the looks department. So why did Alice abandon him and their daughter? What did she want after ten years of silence?

Duet on Fire (Book 2)- Ian and Ruby had problems trying to conceive a child. If that wasn't enough, her ex-lover the current pastor of their church wants her back...

Tangled Chords (Book 3)- Xavier Bell, the poor, ugly duckling has made it rich and his looks have been incredibly improved too. Farrah Knight, hotel heiress had cruelly rejected him in the past but now she needed help. Could Xavier forgive and forget?

Broken Harmony(Book 4)- Aaron Lee, wanted the top job in his family company but he had a moral clause to consider just when Alka, his married ex-girlfriend walks back into his life.

A Past Refrain (Book 5)- Jayce had issues with forgetting Haley Greenwald even though he had a new woman in his life. Will he ever be able to shake his love for Haley?

Perfect Melody (Book 6)- Logan Moore had the perfect wife, Melody but his secretary Sabrina was hell bent on breaking up the family. Sabrina wanted Logan whatever the cost and she had a secret about Melody, that could shatter Melody's image to everyone.

The Bancroft Family Series

Homely Girl (Book 0) - April and Taj were opposites in so many ways. He was the cute, athletic boy that everybody wanted to be friends with. She was the overweight, shy, and withdrawn girl. Do April and Taj have a love that can last a lifetime? Or will time and separate paths rip them apart?

Saving Face (Book 1) - Mount Faith University drama begins with a dead president and several suspects including the president in waiting Ryan Bancroft.

Tattered Tiara (Book 2) - Micah Bancroft is targeted by femme fatale Deidra Durkheim. There are also several rape cases to be solved.

Private Dancer (Book 3) Adrian Bancroft was gutted when he returned to Jamaica and found out that his first and only love Cathy Taylor was a stripper and was literally owned by the menacing drug lord, Nanjo Jones.

Goodbye Lonely (Book 4) - Kylie Bancroft was shy and had to resort to going to confidence classes. How could she win the love of Gareth Beecher, her faculty adviser, a man with a jealous ex-wife in his past and a current mystery surrounding a hand found in his garden?

Practice Run (Book 5) - Marcus Bancroft had many reasons to avoid Mount Faith but Deidra Durkheim was not one of them. Unfortunately, on one of his visits he was the victim of a deliberate hit and run.

Sense of Rumor (Book 6) - Arnella Bancroft was the wild, passionate Bancroft, the creative loner who didn't mind living dangerously; but when a terrible thing happened to her at her friend Tracy's party, it changed her. She found that courting rumors can be devastating and that only the truth could set her free.

A Younger Man (Book 7) - Pastor Vanley Bancroft loved Anita Parkinson despite their fifteen-year age gap, but Anita had a secret, one that she could not reveal to Vanley. To tell him would change his feelings toward her, or force him to give up the ministry that he loved so much.

Just To See Her (Book 8) - Jessica Bancroft had the opportunity to meet her fantasy guy Khaled, he was finally coming to Mount Faith but she had feelings for Clay Reid, a guy who had all the qualities she was looking for. Who would she choose and what about the weird fascination Khaled had for Clay?

The Three Rivers Series

Private Sins (Book 1)- Kelly, the first lady at Three Rivers Church was pregnant for the first elder of her church. Could she keep the secret from her husband and pretend that all was well?

Loving Mr. Wright (Book 2)- Erica saw one last opportunity to ditch her single life when Caleb Wright appeared in her town. He was perfect for her, but what was he hiding?

Unholy Matrimony (Book 3) - Phoebe had a problem, she was poor and unhappy. Her solution to marry a rich man was derailed along the way with her feelings for Charles Black, the poor guy next door.

If It Ain't Broke (Book 4)- Chris Donahue wanted a place in his child's life. Pinky Black just wanted his love. She also wanted him to forget his obsession with Kelly and love her. That shouldn't be so hard? Should it?

Contemporary Romance/Drama

After The End--Torn between two lovers. Colleen married her high school sweetheart, Isaiah, hoping that they would live happily ever after but life intruded and Isaiah disappeared at sea. She found work with the rich and handsome, Enrique Lopez, as a housekeeper and realized that she couldn't keep him at arms length...

Love Triangle: Three Sides To The Story- George, the husband, Marie, the wife and Karen-the mistress. They all get to tell their side of the story.

The Preacher And The Prostitute - Prostitution and the clergy don't mix. Tell that to ex-prostitute, Maribel, who finds herself in love with the Pastor at her church. Can an ex-prostitute and a pastor have a future together?

New Beginnings - Inner city girl Geneva was offered an opportunity of a lifetime when she found out that her 'real' father was a very wealthy man. Her decision to live up-town meant that she had to leave Froggie, her 'ghetto don,' behind. She also found herself battling with her stepmother and battling her emotions for Justin, a suave up-towner.

Full Circle- After graduating from university, Diana wanted to return to Jamaica to find her siblings. What she didn't foresee was that she would meet Robert Cassidy and that both their pasts would be intertwined, and that disturbing questions would pop up about their parentage, just when they were getting close.

Historical Fiction/Romance

The Empty Hammock- Workaholic, Ana Mendez, fell asleep in a hammock and woke up in the year 1494. It was the time of the Tainos, a time when life seemed simpler, but Ana knew that all of that was about to change.

The Pull Of Freedom- Even in bondage the people, freshly arrived from Africa, considered themselves free. Led by Nanny and Cudjoe the slaves escaped the Simmonds' plantation and went in different directions to forge their destiny in the new country called Jamaica.

Jamaican Comedy (Material contains Jamaican dialect)

Di Taxi Ride And Other Stories- Di Taxi Ride and Other Stories is a collection of twelve witty and fast paced short stories. Each story tells of a unique slice of Jamaican life.